Suzannah Dunn

is the author of six other books of fiction: *Darker Days Than Usual, Blood Sugar, Past Caring, Quite Contrary, Venus Flaring* and *Commencing Our Descent*. She lives in Brighton.

Praise for Suzannah Dunn's previous books:

BLOOD SUGAR

'*Blood Sugar* is lit up by images of rare vitality and beauty.'
MAGGIE GEE

'Suzannah Dunn is that rarity among contemporary novelists: a genuine stylist. Her prose is like truffles – rich, rare, dark, but never cloying.'
WENDY PERRIAM

'Suzannah Dunn is a writer with a brilliant touch.'
MALCOLM BRADBURY

PAST CARING

'Poignant and believable... *Past Caring* is a perceptive novel by a writer who skilfully blends the everyday with the fantastic.'
HELEN DUNMORE

'Suzannah Dunn writes in loaded and knowing prose, like a hip Edna O'Brien or Muriel Spark.'
Glasgow Herald

'Suzannah Dunn is a gifted writer.'
POLLY TOYNBEE, *The Times*

Further reviews overleaf

QUITE CONTRARY

'The writing is loaded with vibrant, visual images of so strongly evocative, so poetic a quality that they seem about to burst and to yield up a weight of hidden meaning.'

Literary Review

'A compelling debut novel from a writer steadily gathering critical plaudits for her penetrative eye and unfussy style... a luminous, honest and haunting portrait of a single woman doing a demanding job and trying to stay alive inside as well.'

Scotland on Sunday

'A brilliant portrayal of a young woman coming to terms with her past and present.' *Company*

VENUS FLARING

'The prose is precise, images bloom like bruises or blood drops... compact worlds are contained in the simplest of descriptions. Dunn is a surgeon of the heart, and her observations are sparky.' EITHNE FARRY, *Time Out*

'A writer with a subversive wit that few of her peers can match.' JONATHAN COE

'*Venus Flaring* treats familiar themes to a witty and original overhaul. Dunn marries plot and themes, to create a haunting, melancholy tone perfectly suited to the sense of loss which afflicts even minor characters.'

ALISON WOODHOUSE, *TLS*

'After reading *Venus Flaring* no other book will strike quite so close to your soul... Dunn time after time stuns the reader. This is a vital, refreshing, terrifyingly brilliant novel that demands to be read.' SUSANNA GLASER, *Finetime*

SUZANNAH DUNN

Tenterhooks

Flamingo
An Imprint of HarperCollins*Publishers*

Flamingo
An Imprint of HarperCollins*Publishers*
77–85 Fulham Palace Road,
Hammersmith, London W6 8JB

Published by Flamingo 1999
9 8 7 6 5 4 3 2 1

First published in Great Britain by
Flamingo 1998

ISBN 0 00 655087 8

Set in Sabon by Rowland Phototypesetting Ltd,
Bury St Edmunds, Suffolk

Printed and bound in Great Britain by
Clays Ltd, St Ives plc

CONTENTS

With love and thanks to my editor,
Charlotte Windsor

WHITE GOODS

As we walked down the aisle, he murmured, 'Spinach . . .'

I stopped, leaned over and looked down onto the frozen vegetables. During the two days since the delivery of our freezer I had had numerous fantasies, but none about spinach. Sara Lee, yes; spinach, no. And now Christie was *beginning* with *spinach*? I dipped down into the fizzy chill to scratch my way to greenery; packs of carrots and sweetcorn hissed as they slipped over one another. *Spinach?* I called up. 'Are you *sure*?' By comparison, the sweetcorn looked glamorous.

Above me, behind me, he laughed, '*Never been* more sure.'

But I tried, 'Broccoli florets?' Because *florets* sounded faintly enticing.

'Deceptive.'

I surfaced, enquiringly.

'Thaws to rubber,' he explained.

'How do you know?'

He shrugged, more than necessary, both hands off the moving trolley, *Look, Mum, no hands*. 'I just do. Cauliflower, too. Anything that's not spinach.' A twitch of a smile. 'Which is why I *said spinach*.' Then he said, 'I noticed the mound of Mars Bars,' and managed more of the smile.

Those Mars Bars would have been hard to miss: the only contents, so far, of the freezer. 'A girl needs her luxuries.'

His eyes dropped wider: he is the only person whom I

know who has eyes like trap doors. He said, 'And I was so sure that it was *greens* that a girl needed.'

I returned to the matter of the frozen spinach, which, I found, existed in two forms: solid blocks, the size of paperback books; or pellets, packed loosely into cushion-sized bags. A block would be slow to thaw, and then would swamp us in spinach: a problem to which there is no solution (spinach sandwiches?). I had never had a freezer, but I knew the rule, I knew never to refreeze: everyone knows that to thaw food is to disturb the undead. I reached down into the freezer. Although they were impractical, I liked the feel of the solid blocks, but they were made of leaf spinach: a leaf which is not in fact a leaf but a length of vivid green silk to make bobbins of our front teeth. I turned my attention to the pellets: *chopped* spinach, which I recognized as a euphemism for minced. Silently vowing that spinach was the only minced vegetable that I would allow before my ninetieth birthday, I hauled a pack from the icy-fluffy depths.

Three weeks later, three weekly shopping trips later, and our frozen food supply is three feet deep. On several occasions we have filled a saucepan with those frosted pellets of moss, and hey presto . . . Hey presto, thawed spinach. But Christie thinks of something, he always thinks of something, he saves the day with a curry or a lasagne. By contrast, I am quick to despair. In my hands, thawed spinach remains thawed spinach, becomes nothing better than warm spinach. The freezer has not made a cook of me. But Christie can cook, and now our lives have become like other people's lives, with proper meals, like clockwork. Our freezer needs feeding, but this is fun: we drive to a hangar of a supermarket, spin a trolley around stacks of food, pick up whatever we fancy and then pay by card, which is not like paying at all. And the freezer more than repays us: a lift of the lid to find the fruits of our labours. I have heard that the hitch is a loss of flavour over time, but I am sure that I can live with that.

But now I have to do something because the food is thawing below me in the kitchen, slowly losing its lifeblood of ice as I float warm here in my bed. A moment ago, opening my eyes, I turned to my clock to find that the digital display was wholly black – hollow. I ran my hand down the wall for the switch for my lamp; the switch snapped down but seemed to fall short – nothing, no power. We are deep into the night: the moon is high, shrunk to a pearl; the silence is as thorough as new, heavy snow. I am softened by sleep and can only wait for my clock to open its green eyes, to show me how the power cut is merely a momentary failure, a flicker, a mistake. But nothing. There is nothing that I can do to fix this. Time for damage limitation: I will have to leave my bed and go downstairs with blankets for the freezer.

Slipping over the mattress, I try to keep the duvet level, to avoid any pull on Christie. As soon as I am clear, I pause to listen hard for him, for his silence. In two minutes' time, I will be back here and turning back into my own sleep, gathering up the remainder of my sleep to see me through to morning. I do not even bother with my dressing gown. How odd that we close our door although there is no one else in the house to keep us from, to keep from us. The opening door cracks into the hush of our room. But still nothing from Christie. I cannot see his face, only the top of his head, his hair: he is hunched into the duvet. Out there in the hallway the moonshine is pooled on the top few stairs. Pulling hard on the airing cupboard door, I tense for the snap of the plastic nub from its socket in the frame. When I was a child, my parents had special uses for the airing cupboard: a treasure trove for our birthday and Christmas presents, and a nest for the incubation of our slightly mushy Easter eggs. A winter holiday home, too, for my tortoise; the place where, every year, very slowly, he died, sort of, then sort of came alive again.

Nowadays I have friends who are diligent about bulbs: they plant bulbs in bowls, plant the bowls in their airing cupboards, and then they wait, all winter. But I am suspicious of shoots, stiff and pallid; they do not seem natural, somehow, not in an airing cupboard. My own warm shelves, in front of me, are slopped with underwear: straps, frills, bows, mostly washing powder white, nothing flash, because when I was young enough for experiments with underwear, I was too poor, and then, later, when I had money, I had lost my nerve, I had grown up. And I have never caught up: underwear remains a language that I do not speak well, in which I am untidy and tight-lipped. I get by, with a rather teen-bra look.

The blankets are on the top shelf, so my hands flutter over the underwear and then scale several shelves of towels. Warm, even smelling warm, these towels have a very thin crust, they are slightly dried and hardened from laundering. They came in batches as house-warming presents from relatives, who, I suspect, had asked the advice of my parents; and here they are, in the centre of my house, still warm, still warming. When they came, I took my old towels to a charity shop. My old towels had been *very* old. But then these new towels began to unnerve me. They had come in kindness, a kind of kindness, because my family knew that I had always had to make do, but I worried that they were a conspiracy to turn me normal, to turn my head and make me houseproud. I remember my dad saying, *All I want is to see you married.* My mum is the only person whom I know to use the word *slattern.* Once, she referred to a local girl who had lived with and then left her boyfriend as *soiled goods.* My bed linen is my own because my relatives were unsure whether they should buy anything for the bed of two unmarried people. I was happy to buy my own: I caught up on bed linen in a big way, in my belief that bed linen should *be linen.* No cotton/polyester mixes. Why was I so serious about this, when my underwear remains the equivalent of flannelette fitted sheets?

The blankets drop one by one from the shelf, their folds wriggling from my arms. I strain behind my bundle to kick the cupboard door shut, then waddle to the stairs. The towels, fattening and breathing their fragrance into my airing cupboard, those house-warming towels makes me think of my sister. Belinda *was* married, but I do not know what she is now: single, divorced, separated, or simply sulking? She was married for nine months and has now been back home for six. Like a character from a book or a film, a character from the Deep South. Except that she wears Snoopy slippers, and has never lived anywhere but Hatfield. I was told that the marriage *didn't work*, as if it was a dud among the many electrical appliances that had come gift-wrapped to the wedding reception. Mum says that Belinda *doesn't-want-to-talk-about-it.* If I was Belinda, I would not even want to *think* about it: Freddie was her first boyfriend, when she was fourteen, and she stuck with him for twelve years. He was a nice boy, he must have seemed like a good idea at the time, but for twelve years?

Mum had only one comment for me: Belinda and Freddie had been *more like brother and sister* – she did not say *than lovers* – and then, when they married, *he wasn't quite what she had expected*. Which could mean anything. They had not lived together before they married, and their relationship was the only one that I have ever known for which *going out together* was an accurate description. Whenever they saw each other, they went to the cinema or to restaurants, or sometimes further afield on holidays. I was around, on and off, for seven of their twelve years, and I am not quite sure that I ever saw them together without their coats; I am not too sure that they ever saw *each other* without their coats. They were forever turning through the front door, a huge and unbalanced version of one of those weather vanes which shows a man or a woman for rain or shine. In their case, always rain: from my room at the top of the stairs I would sense how the hallway flickered with their red-tipped noses and shook with the clapping of cold from their mitts. Belinda has always been the same: my little sister, she was older than her years by my two; but whenever she moved forward with me (finding a boyfriend, gaining an allowance, drinking Snowballs), she stuck. With make-up, even: she began young and daring, choosing eyeshadows which reminded me of the underside of leaves, but then she stuck with them. Her eyelids are still like leaves switched and splayed in the wind when she settles for the evening with a TV dinner in her lap.

Sometimes I have to go home for some reason or other, and when I was last there, I took a detour from the bathroom to peep into her bedroom. I was shocked by what I saw: *gonks*, a colony on her windowsill. I was shocked, even, that I knew what they were, that I knew the name for them.

Listening for her heavy tread on the stairs, I crossed the room in a few quick paces and peered down onto their forced smiles, the smiles that had been forced into the plastic to make their faces. I did not fondle their hair, which was nylon, lurid, and frayed, although I was fairly sure that part of the point of gonks was to fondle their hair. I had had a gonk or two when I was a child, when everyone had had a few, so I knew that the main point of them was to bring luck. During exams, our gonks stood on guard by the obsolete inkwells of our old desks. But in exams they failed Belinda badly, her teachers failed her badly, her reports were jagged with Es and Fs. Not that this caused trouble for her, because Mum and Dad would tell her that what mattered was happiness. Now Belinda's gonks have another use: they occupy the void on the sill which, for twelve years, had displayed the faces of the happy couple in frames. The grinning gonks manage fair impressions of the two missing faces and even of Belinda's yellow hair which has sometimes been only faintly real.

Because she had had Freddie for twelve years, she seemed to have lost track of her childhood friends, and made no new ones. A neighbour's child played the role of bridesmaid. Because Dad had died, Belinda arranged for Freddie's father to give her away, which made less than no sense. I wonder if he gave her back, I wonder if he drove her home when the marriage was over, because how else did she cross town with her belongings? She and Freddie had no car, and Mum has never learned to drive. Back home, there is a portable television in her bedroom; this is the extent of her independence, now. Which she never seems to use. Because Mum likes her company. Belinda likes home comforts and Mum likes company: this is how the situation works. The only change in their relationship happened ten years ago, when Belinda started work: the allowance switched, no longer paid by Mum and Dad to Belinda but by Belinda to Mum and Dad. Belinda has had the same job for ten years: receptionist at the local leisure centre. *Leisure* is ironic: even the entrance hall is hard work, with the machine-gun fire of the turnstiles, the echoes of pot shots from the squash courts, and the chemical warfare of chlorine. Presumably she earns very little, but apart from Mum's allowance to cover food and bills, she has no expenses: no house, no car. So, she has always had money for the pictures, for pizzas, for presents, for exactly the expenses which I have always found a strain. Sufficient for holidays, even: her talk was always of *booking* holidays, my talk has always been of *saving* for holidays.

Here in the kitchen are several unpaid bills, dumped in the fruit bowl until they turn red. In this darkness, they are as luminous as the moon. Christie and I share the bills, but he covers our other expenses: everything for the house and the car, meals in restaurants, drinks with friends, the eventual holidays. He paid for this freezer. I can survive, I have managed to keep my business running through the recession when the trade in old clocks, antique clocks, has been slow – a trade which took years to learn, a business which took years to build, and which my parents considered as an odd choice for a woman because, in their opinion, the only clock which should concern a woman is the biological one. But there is no way that I could afford to live alone, or not to live like this. None of my friends lives alone, now. And lately most of them have married. Even my best friend Sarah has a shrine on her mantelpiece: three framed photos, close-ups of bride and groom on backdrops of Rolls-Royce and cake. She took a year to plan the details of her wedding, down to her under-wear. To his underwear, too, probably. The low point was the fuss over the colour of the napkins, but she told me that, 'Napkins *have to be* a colour, a decision *has to be made, someone* has to make the decision, and I'm determined that the someone should be *me.*' Her three photos are talismans and whenever I go around to see her, to try to talk to her, I see those photos and I am cowed.

My problem seems so simple. Why is there no simple solution? The problem is that whenever I see Christie, nothing happens to me. And, once upon a time, something would have happened. Something has stopped. I have a memory from school, from a chemistry or biology lesson, something biochemical and messy and unlike my beloved physics: a diagram on the blackboard, a row of molecules or cells or something, made of heads on stems; and the heads switched towards water, they strained towards water. The teacher told us that they were hydrophilous: '*Hydro*, water; *philous*, loving.' I know that I am no longer drawn to Christie, I have stopped being moved by him, I am no longer in love with him. What I do not know is if this matters: is love a luxury? Can I stay, loveless like this? Faint-hearted? Or should I leave? But if I leave, I lose him, he loses me, we lose the life that we live so well together. But if I stay, is this a life? Am I living a lie? Am I lying to him?

An old, old story: I have everything, but something is missing. What is missing in me is tenderness: the heads of my cells have stopped turning on their stems, but still, there should be tenderness; a little give in those stems, a wry incline of those heads. A sway to echo the punch-drunkenness of that initial passion. How ironic: the illicit lovers, more like brother and sister. Sometimes when I am alone, I wind my way around this house, from room to room finding furniture, appliances, ornaments for which we planned, or which we tried to deny ourselves, or saved hard to afford; and those that were impulses, or argued over, or mistakes. These memories pinch, surprise me sometimes to tears, but they fail to move me. There seems to be no way forward, and I know that there is no going back.

Now I hear the kisses of Christie's soles on the tiles behind me. They stop, and the blankets seem to limbo up from the floor where I had laid them, one of them nestling around my shoulders. He turns me around to him, into the warmth of him, and with him, back into darkness, back to bed. Presumably he thinks that I am sleepwalking, as I have done on several occasions now. Jokingly, he has referred to my nocturnal restlessness as *failing to sleep off your late, louche lunches.* Sometimes I wish that I could sleep off my whole life. As he leads me away from the thawing freezer, I want to tell him, but I am so very tired and no words come.

SYNC

For Katy Rensten

For hours, the moon has been rolling around the windows of this minibus like a pin-ball. And now we are passing roofs which are slick with moonshine. These roofs are new to our journey: for hours we were on a motorway, in the middle of nowhere, overtaken by vehicles with unblinking yellow eyes and snappy indicators. In the headlamp-splashed darkness, my friends' faces were dilated to pitch and catch conversation over the noise of the engine, the rolling tide of tyres. For a while, now, though, everyone has been quiet; even Mr Stanford, whose busy eyes, in his high narrow mirror, have become smaller and more level. The only other open eyes are those of the only other boy on this field trip, Lawrence; the view from one of the windows licks through the shiny surface of them. With the appearance of the roofs, I realize that we are nearly there, and my heart sinks. What is it that they say, in planes? *We are commencing our descent.*

Hours and hours of engine vibration have drummed my thighs into the wooden slats of the bench, but I am further pinned down by Rachel, who is slumped asleep on me. A hairsprayed sprig of her hair lisps into my ear with every bump and turn of the minibus. One of her hands has dropped between her thigh and mine, and lies on both, open. On the tops of her upwardly-curled fingers, the thin crescent moons of her nails are oddly shadowed: she has painted them, because we are away from school, where nail polish is forbidden. Mr Stanford brakes, pauses behind a badly-parked car for a chain of oncoming traffic to pass; Rachel presses harder onto my shoulder, sinks further. There has been a lot of this, the stopping and sinking, like a drunken dance, since we turned from the motorway into these towns of crowded chip shops and dark banks, towns so much smaller than our own. An empty can growls again on the floor. I cannot reach with my feet to stop it. Lawrence's eyes peel from the window and follow the can, they are wide with worry, but he makes no move, his hands in prayer between his thighs.

Susie's head looks like a sculpture in butter: no shadows, and her hair, face, eyebrows and eyelashes the same colour. On her wedding-ring finger is the ring that Nathan Harper gave her: a *staying-together ring*, in her words. Next to her, Trina and Avril are propping up each other's dozes – very different dozes: Trina's face is hard, all chin and frown; Avril's has slipped into a smile. This is all of us: me and Rachel, Susie, Trina, Avril, and Lawrence. And Mr Stanford, of course, unfortunately; in his opinion, he is one of us. There are so few of us because this field trip is for biology and hardly anyone wants to do biology in the sixth form. Suddenly, I see that Mr Stanford's eyes have been looking for mine.

'Nearly there,' he says to me, via the mirror, then laughs. 'I'm desperate for a pint.'

One-of-the-boys. I shut my eyes, to shut him up.

The only place in the world that I dread more than *nearly there* is *there*. Rachel and I tried everything to avoid this trip: marine biology for five days of our half term holiday, five days in February on a peninsula in South Wales.

We began by knocking politely on the door marked *Biology*

Head and then explaining to Mr Bennett that we wanted to go with our English class to Stratford. Which was true if only because *King Lear* is not quite five days long. Both trips take place during the same half term holiday each year, because there has never before been an overlap between biology and English. Mr Bennett's view was that the field trip was necessary for our biology, but that Stratford was an optional extra for English. Which is not quite what our English teachers said but – being English teachers – they were too liberal to cause a fuss. So then Rachel and I had to come up with another hitch.

We decided that we could not miss any of *The Crucible* rehearsals, two of which were scheduled for this week. This was too much for Mr Bennett, who sent us to Mr Dene, the Headmaster. Mr Dene said that all we had to do in our roles was scream. We informed him that there was much more to our roles than simple screams – that we had to scream at the correct moments and with the correct intensity. In our defence we called one of the English teachers, who was directing the play, and she did her best, but Mr Dene – being Mr Dene – refused to listen to her.

So then Rachel marched into his office and did not stop until she was in the middle, where she hooked her hair behind her ears to show that she meant business and said to him, 'Look,' *I'll be straight with you,* 'we just don't want to go, okay?'

This *okay* was her mistake, because from behind his desk he bellowed, 'No, it is *not* okay,' and went on, 'if you refuse to go on this field trip, then you will be unprepared for your exams and I will refuse to allow you to take them.'

I stepped forward from the doorway to join Rachel, and

explained calmly, 'Mr Dene, marine biology is one of our options; in the exam, we have to write essays on four of six options. So, we can easily avoid marine biology.' I had done my homework.

But my mistake was to have mentioned options, and ease. Why did I do this? I know very well that Mr Dene's whole life is about the destruction of our options and ease. I think that I may even have smiled, slightly, which, if I did, was even more stupid of me.

Mr Dene addressed Rachel, which people usually do: parents and teachers, they all direct their arguments to Rachel, often looking at the four earrings that she has in both ears, as if this justifies their shouting, as if the earrings are blocking her ears. 'You will go,' he yelled, leaning over his desk, 'because I say so.'

Rachel muttered, 'Wonderful philosophy of education,' but stepped backwards to the door. I could not believe that she was giving in so readily. But I followed her, I had to follow her; if I had not followed, I would have been left behind. At the door, though, she turned our defeat into a threat: 'We'll go,' she told him, and cocked a cold smile onto her face, 'but, believe me, we don't have to like it.'

And so here we are, not liking it: I did not choose biology so that I could study whelks; I chose biology because I was interested in people. I wanted to follow the intense and precise activities beneath our skin. I love the logic of biology: in bodies, everything has a time and place. This is why biology is so easy to learn, for all the intricacies. Because I only have to think, as long as I think very carefully: what is needed, here, and what happens next, what *has* to happen next?

Unlike those other favourite subjects of mine, literature and history, which are made of people's schemes, mistakes, runnings amok. But the logic of bodies is different from the meaningless logic of maths or of the other school sciences, chemistry and physics. Biology makes sense: I can hold the bits in my hands, if I want, if I need, and they are the means to an end, an end which is real, which is *life*. In the chemistry labs, the plastic models of molecules look like starships given away in packets of breakfast cereal. And physics: I remember one lesson, on inertia, and I suppose that inertia is real in a sense, but not *really* real; physics was a lot of ticker tape.

But my biology has to be human; or, at a push, mammalian, and then only because of the similarity of their little bodies to ours, their skulls and spines. I have no interest in animals which drag shells or lay eggs, and I have even less interest in plants, those stacks of starchy cells which soak up whatever is dropped on them. There are whole textbooks that I never open: *The Plant World*, *The World of Invertebrates*. Unfortunately, marine biology is made from the very worst of both worlds, animal and plant: animals that are no more than plants, and plants that are more like animals. All of them are bits of slime that stick to and hide in rocks.

Three days ago, I despaired and took matters into my own hands: I went to the doctor and lied that I was ill. She asked questions about my appetite, kneaded my neck with her fingertips, pressed her cold stethoscope to my bared chest, found nothing and diagnosed a virus.

I explained, 'But I'm going to a peninsula for a biology field trip in three days' time.'

She reassured me, 'Oh, I'm sure you'll be fine.'

I hurried, 'But what if I'm not?'

She frowned, smiled, told me to come back if I did not improve. So, I did, yesterday, to tell her that I was worse. She pulled down my lower eyelids, looked into my mouth, frowned into my face and asked me, 'Do you have anything on your mind, at the moment?'

'Yes, the biology field trip.'

She smiled. 'Fresh air and exercise: you'll be fine.'

'But what if I'm not?' I urged.

She soothed, 'Don't worry.'

We seemed to be at cross purposes.

Then she laughed, genuinely happily. 'You'll survive.'

Survival: I love the perfection of human biology but also, and perhaps more so, the flaws; I love the possibility of flaws, which cannot exist in the other sciences where everything either *is* or is *not*. I love the ways that bodies can overcome their problems. I love the mysteries, too, the unmapped depths of bodies. There is a brain injury that causes people to try to have sex with anyone or anything. Which means that there is a biological basis for inhibition, that even self-control is biological.

We have survived the first full day of field work. The schedule pinned to our dormitory door tells us that, now, having had our *Dinner*, we are *Free* until *Lights Out* at eleven o'clock. This seems expertly cruel: we are free, but there is nothing to do and nowhere to go. Before we came here, Mr Stanford told us that he would drive us to local pubs, and we decided that an evening with him was better than nothing. But arriving here yesterday, parking in the courtyard, in the darkness, he hit something and tore off the back bumper. So now the minibus is awaiting the attentions of the local garage man, who is due sometime much later in the week. When we whined to Mr Stanford, this evening, over dinner, that we had nothing to do, he laughed and suggested that we take advantage of the library. This mention of the library was to flatter Jim, the Course Leader, who was sitting with him – this morning, during our Briefing (*09.05, Briefing, Prefab no. 2*), Jim had fantasized long and loud over the library. He had told us that the library was excellent, rare, renowned, so that people came from all over the country.

Rachel whispered in my ear, 'Yeah, my mum is always nipping down here.'

Jim must have heard, because he looked at her earrings and stressed, '*Marine biologists.*'

He is a marine biologist, which, for some reason, seems to impress Mr Stanford. Not us, though: one day here and we have discovered that marine biologists are the lowest form of life. At lunch time, Mr Stanford owned up that he would have liked to have become a marine biologist. We think that he would like to be Jim, climbing over rocks with the wind in his hair. We think that Mr Stanford has been tampering with his hair today so that he looks like Jim. He is happy here, and has made no effort to hide this from us. He has a drinking buddy in Jim, which we know because Avril overheard Jim's promise of *a hot toddy or two tonight in my room*. And, more importantly for him, he has found someone to fancy, someone called Janet who is here to research for a Ph.D. in algae. And she *looks* as if she is here to research for a Ph.D. in algae. Avril saw Mr Stanford turn from Jim to Janet, heard him ask her, 'Janet? A hot toddy or two, later?' He has plans, now; he cares even less about us, he makes no pretence, now.

When he laughed and told us to spend the evening in the library, I was only amazed that anyone could laugh anywhere in the vicinity of that meal. We had been called to dinner by an electric bell, like a fire alarm, which jangled the courtyard where we were trying to remove our waterproofs. We had come back late from what Jim called *the field*; he had kept us too long *in the field* and then taken us, in our waterproofs, into Prefab no. 2 for a late Debriefing. When the alarm rang, Mr Stanford announced, cheerfully, 'Dinner.'

Avril complained, 'That noise! Can't we have a gong or something?'

Mr Stanford said, 'No.'

In the dining-room, we had to queue with various staff and researchers for food, which was served in individual portions on metal trays. According to one of the cooks, the stew was lamb and the vegetable was swede. I asked her, 'Is there any vegetarian?'

She said, 'None in Pembrokeshire that I know of.'

I walked carefully to Mr Stanford with my runny portion and said, 'But I'm vegetarian.'

He said, 'No you're not.'

I told him, 'Yes I am.'

He laughed. 'No you're not: humans are omnivorous.'

I ignored this. 'I'm *vegetarian*.'

Suddenly humourless again, he said, 'But if you were vegetarian, you would have thought about this, you would have told me before we came away.'

I had to think quickly. 'I've converted. There has to be a moment of conversion, and mine is now, with this lamb.'

'Scrag end,' corrected Trina, coming over, grimly cheerful, with her own tray.

Mr Stanford said, 'Tough.'

Trina agreed, 'You can say that again,' and demonstrated, poking a piece with her knife.

I told him, 'I'm not touching this, or anything like this; and if I starve, you're responsible.'

He fizzled into exasperation, hissed to the ceiling, 'Why are girls so *fussy*?' Then he shouted through the hatch, 'Is there any vegetarian?'

And a voice came back, 'There's a banana.'

So I had swede and banana, which I mashed together.

And now we are in our room for the evening; we have all crowded into the room which belongs to me, Rachel, and Susie. Even Lawrence, who was found in the corridor by Trina when she was coming from the room which she shares with Avril. According to her, he was pretending to read the bulletin board which is pinned with local maps and posters of seaweed. She told us this after pulling him into our room and announcing, 'Look who I've found: *Loz*.' She always calls him Loz.

We had temporarily overlooked Lawrence, in our self-pity. We apologized profusely and offered him a toddy; we have our own, a toddy but not hot, a quarter bottle of Scotch which Rachel was clever enough to buy from the supermarket on her way to school yesterday. We passed the bottle to Lawrence and he swigged, but appeared not to swallow and has declined all further offers. He is sitting on the end of the bed next to the door, which is mine. His knees are prominent.

Susie left the room ten minutes ago to phone Nathan. We can hear her on the pay phone at the end of our corridor, but her murmurs make no sense to us, they are little question marks to hook and hold his attention. On her pillow is an unfinished letter to him. Rachel, lounging on the floor, has been lying in wait for my gaze which she snares now in a conspiratorial smile.

'What?' I ask, wary, my hand pausing in the box of breakfast crunch, which is our only treat because we have already eaten our week's supply of chocolate.

Holding my gaze, she reclines, suddenly switches her attention to the top sheet of Susie's letter.

'Don't,' I am serious but I laugh, I am so serious that I have to laugh.

But without taking her eyes from the letter, she raises her eyebrows. 'Is it folded carefully away, or is it here on her pillow for everyone to see?' As her eyes move over the words, her teeth come slowly onto her lower lip to hold down a smile.

So that now she has me: 'What?' I have to know, to coax her, 'What does she say?'

The eyes widen to confront me. 'I'm not breaking Susie's confidence,' she complains, mock-indignant.

I tut her away, but then the letter hovers in front of me in Rachel's hand.

I shake my head.

So she places the letter back onto the pillow and tells me the truth. 'She says nothing; *We arrived here* . . . that kind of stuff.' And hums a laugh, 'Or so far, because I stopped before the juicy bits.'

Avril peeps over her crossword puzzle book, '*Are* there juicy bits?'

Rachel turns on her. 'Don't you tell her that I read this.'

The door opens, slightly increasing the volume but not the sense of Susie's words, and Trina hurries into the room. 'There's a notice in there,' she wails, '*Do not flush away sanitary dressings.*' Looking around us, she emphasizes, 'Sanitary *dressings.*'

I wonder, 'Any relation to salad dressings?'

Her gaze catches momentarily on Lawrence, 'Oh, sorry, Loz.'

Rachel complains, 'Shut the door, it's freezing.'

It is not freezing in here, but our bodies bear the memory of a long cold day on the shore and now shiver in response to the mere opening of doors. If anything, it is too warm in here. The block of dormitories is new, and seems to be built from static.

Shutting the door, Trina complains, 'It's so cold that I can't even face going for a fag.' We have to go outside to smoke; the building is fitted with smoke detectors. She stomps across the room and thumps the window. 'Has anyone managed to open this yet?'

Avril says, 'I don't think it's supposed to open, it's like a porthole. Because of all the water around here.'

We all turn to her. And I check, 'You think the water comes *up to here?*'

'Well, *possibly.*'

For a moment we listen, and hear something like a tube train far below us.

'Anyway,' I tell Trina, 'those cigarettes are off.'

No one disputes this. The cigarettes are stale. I have never had a stale cigarette before. I have never had very many cigarettes at all; I smoke only when I am under stress and there are no other options, no sugar, no alcohol, no music, no Mike or Jamie, and no laughs from Rachel. The stale cigarettes came from Rachel, who disappeared from the courtyard during the confusion of waterproofs removal. She returned twenty minutes late for dinner. Sliding next to me on the bench, with a wild wrinkle of her nose in the direction of my mashed meal, she nudged my attention to her hidden hands: beneath the table, three packets of cigarettes, *sixty*; I swallowed a wave of nausea. And interrogated her, 'Where have you been?'

To keep Mr Stanford's attention at bay, she faked interest in my plate while she whispered, 'The local sort of corner shop.'

Local? So there was hope, there was *a locality*.

'Where?'

She inclined her head, slightly, 'About a mile in that direction,' then laughed briefly, 'the direction of inland.'

'So,' I urged, 'there's a village or something?'

'No, nothing.' She was wriggling to slot the packets into her pockets. I kept watch on Mr Stanford for her. Which was a mistake: he was carefully in conversation with Janet the Algae, their heads low and close, but when this composure exploded with a laugh, his gaze came quickly to mine. I smiled beautifully, and he looked away.

I returned my attention to Rachel. 'But you said *corner shop*.'

'I said *sort of* corner shop. It *would be* a corner shop if there was a corner.' She winced her apologies, 'It's just a shop, Jenny.'

I thrashed my meal with my fork. 'And you've missed dinner.'

She frowned down into the sticky mess, then looked up

into my despondent face and widened her eyes to make her point.

Reluctantly, I smiled. 'Yes, but you'll starve.'

She shrugged this off, 'We have that box of crunchy mix.'

I did not say, *Why no chocolate? Why sixty cigarettes and no Aero?* Because she was right, she did the right thing: the final disastrous touch to the week would be a few extra inches on our hips.

Now Trina is crashing back across our brittle, smoke-free room. 'Well, if the ciggies are off . . .' Her boots crunch our spillages of cereal. She leaves the door open as she hurries into her own room. Returning, she asks, 'Want one?' but immediately turns away to close our door very firmly. There is a plain brown envelope in one hand, a few pinhead pills slipping down over the flap into the palm of her other hand. They line up like beads of mercury in the main crease, the main channel of her palm.

I want to know, 'What are they?'

She extracts one in a pincer of index finger and thumb, and pushes it between her lips. 'Anti-depressants,' the reply comes slightly sticky, 'my mum's.'

Rachel sits taller. 'What do they do?'

The pills slam back down onto one another in the envelope, and Tina heads for Susie's vacant bed. 'Cure depression, I suppose.' Reclining, she holds the envelope high, keeping open the offer.

Avril doubts, '*One* of them will cure depression?'

Lawrence looks exactly how he looks in class: interested, but in facts rather than fun.

'*Well, no,*' Trina wails her irritation with Avril. 'But they can't make me feel *worse* than how I feel now.'

Rachel stretches to the volume control on the tape recorder because the tape has reached 'Changes', her favourite track. 'So why do *you* have them?' she shouts over David Bowie, her voice further strained by her stretch.

Trina's eyes slot towards her. 'I nicked them, of course.'

Rachel dismisses this with a shake of her head. 'No, I mean, won't she notice?'

Trina gives up, chucks the envelope on to the floor. 'My mum notices nothing,' she tells the ceiling.

Rachel's eyes slide to me on a smile. 'Wouldn't I love to have that kind of mum.'

I tell her, 'Do you know that Jamie has tried some heroin?'

Apparently too weary to speak, she widens her eyes, *Really?*

'Sniffed,' I inform her, 'not injected.' And therefore not addictive, or so he told me. 'Says it was like lying in a warm bath.'

'A warm bath,' she repeats, and seems to breathe in as she speaks, her eyes misting.

Avril says, 'The showers on Mr Stanford's corridor are better than ours: I went to explore. No mould on *his* wall.'

Rachel coughs a laugh. 'He'd *love* some mould, Av, it's biology.'

Trina tells us, 'H is for losers.'

Avril's incomprehension tightens into a frown, which she tries to feel her way through, begins by mouthing, '*H* . . .'

Rachel flips back the top of the cigarette packet, and muses, 'You hang around with the wrong kind of people, Jennifer Jordan.'

'So do you.'

'I'm older.' This is our joke, because she is twenty-two days

30

older than me. 'And one day you're going to end up in a lot
of trouble,' which is another joke of ours because it is our
teachers' and parents' favourite declaration. A declaration
that is intended for Rachel, primarily, but which seems to
reach me by osmosis.

I indicate the packet in her hands: 'Not in here,' I remind
her, 'the smoke alarm.'

'I'm only sniffing.' She draws the cigarette along the length
of her smile, and lingers on the tip, where she inhales dramatically.

Then we both join in with Bowie for, 'Ch-ch-ch-
ch-changes . . .'

When we have finished this, our favourite line, there is
silence; this is a hard line to follow, and anyway there is
nothing new to say.

After a while, I ask around the room, 'Do *any* of us *need*
to do marine biology?'

Trina mutters, 'Like fuck.'

Avril agrees, 'Never ever.'

Rachel adds, 'And I think that we can speak for Susie, too.'

Susie is taking biology because she wants to be a nurse.
Trina wants to be a physio: *manhandling rugby players*, she
tells us and we do not know if she is serious. No one knows
what Avril wants to do. Rachel's reasons for biology are the
same as mine. We became friends through biology, on the
back bench in O level, from where we would counter Mr
Bennett's descriptions of flawless function with questions
about diseases and their cures.

Suddenly phlegm whinnies in Lawrence's throat. 'Well . . .'
his voice, in our room, sounds odd; seems to sound odd to
him, too, because he blinks convulsively, his eyes like moths,

and his mouth thins but falls short of a smile. He tries again, rushes, 'I want to be a vet, so I have to study animals, but not . . .' and he fades.

'Not whelks,' Rachel says for him, turning to him.

'No.' His eyes fix on her, seem to implore.

'Of course not whelks,' she reassures him, before returning to the rest of us to announce, 'so, the Nobel Prize for marine biology is awarded to Trina.'

Trina struggles up onto her elbows and whines a quizzical, 'My arse.'

Rachel explains, 'Nautical Night': Trina's favourite club, once a month on a boat on the Thames.

Day Three, and Jim has finished our Briefing, has told us what we have to do today: we have to mark square metres on a rock face and note the distribution of barnacles within this grid. He did not apologize; on the contrary, he seemed to think that his little exercise would appeal to us, that this would seem like a good way to spend a day. Yesterday, when we were supposed to be probing rock pools, I wandered and came across Lawrence. He was crouched behind a boulder, lighting a new cigarette from the previous one. When he was dabbing the old stub onto a barnacle, he saw me. His mouth was so busy with the second cigarette that he could only manage to hoist his eyebrows in greeting. I was so shocked that I could think of nothing to say but a sympathetic, 'They're stale.'

He exhaled, sighed smokily, 'They're better than nothing.'

I bumped and tottered back over the rocks to Rachel and asked her, 'Did you give Lawrence some of those horrid cigarettes?'

She looked up from her rock pool, and raked through her wind-whipped and salt-stiffened hair. 'Yes, a few, although he tried to say no.' Her frown meshed with the streaks of her hair. 'Why?' Breathless with the sea breeze, I laughed helplessly as I informed her, 'He's behaving appallingly, up there: smoking, and burning barnacles.'

She stood up, grinned slowly, and reached into her mouth for a limpet of chewing gum which she dropped into the rock pool before she murmured appreciatively, 'Loz unleashed.'

Now Jim is slamming through the swing door into the courtyard, keen to lead us down to the shore for another day of excitement. But every day we are allowed a few minutes before we leave, in which to zip and Velcro ourselves into our layers and to fetch anything that we have forgotten. Then Jim will bark, 'Notebooks?' Because according to him, the notebook is the indispensable tool of the marine biologist: a *pocket stiff notebook*, in his words. A *pocket stiff*, in ours. As we leave the bench to follow him, my pocket stiff falls open onto the floor. Bending down, I scan the displayed page, the words which, on our first day, we had been told to copy from Jim's blackboard: *Supplementary fauna key: Limpets; if no groove, look into shell mouth; if mother-of-pearl, then top-shell, if no mother-of-pearl, then winkle.* Beneath this I had scrawled, 'Ziggy Stardust', Trina's favourite Bowie track, which she sang for hours in the minibus. I pick up the book by the cover and the pages spin to today's copied words, the chart on which we are supposed to record the distribution of barnacles: *on bare rock, on weeded rock, in rock pools, in crevices, on pebbles, under boulders, on plants, on animals.* Across the top of this chart I have written 'Suffragette City', which is my own favourite.

I am going to check on Rachel. When I came into the Briefing and told Mr Stanford that she was too ill to leave her bed, he turned from me without a word and hurried across the courtyard to our dormitory block. That was five minutes ago, and he has not yet returned. During the night, I woke twice, briefly, barely, to see Rachel away from her bed. The first time, she was standing by the window, stooped over something in her hands. She was pearly in the overspill of floodlight from the courtyard. Her T-shirt, the hem flopped on the tops of her thighs, turned her into a child's drawing of a girl in a dress: the triangular dress and long lines for legs. But no colour: all of her was pearly, even her eyes. And the earrings: the show of earrings reduced to nothing, to polite pearls. She was drooping, and then came the sound that told me what she was doing: the smash of a pill through a membrane of silver foil.

I asked, 'You okay?'

She seemed unsurprised to hear me, but this apparent calm could have been simply the careful slowness of her turn towards me. A small sound came despite her closed mouth; not quite a groan. Then she made an effort to elaborate: 'I'm having a baby.'

Period pain. In reply, I made a similar sound, but lower and heavier: the appropriate show of sympathy. Then sleep must have washed up over me again and pulled me away.

The second time I opened my eyes, she was coming into the room; and behind her, the corridor buzzed with the far away roar of water into a toilet bowl.

'You okay?' I checked again.

But by now she was more resigned, throwing me an almost tuneful, 'Uh-huh,' as she crossed the room to her bed. I heard the rasp of drawn bedclothes, then the wince of bedsprings beneath her.

This morning she lay in bed while we moved around her. She moved only her eyes, which were no longer pearls but dry pink petals. I was followed by them as I rushed around the room, finding my clothes and throwing back questions. 'So what do I tell Mr Stanford?'

'That I'm ill.'

'Yes, but do I say *with what*?'

'Up to you.'

'Have you had any painkillers this morning?'

'Three.'

'Will you be okay?'

'Fine.'

'Sure?'

'Sure.'

Mr Stanford had not seemed to want to know the details, had said nothing before he turned and hurried away. But now, as I come through the door to the dormitory block, the corridor is full of his voice, a voice which washes over the walls, 'Well, I simply do not believe that an aspirin or two won't fix you.'

Rachel's voice burns into his. 'How would *you* know? And I've *had* an-aspirin-or-two, in fact I've had *three*.'

Turning the corner, I see them in the doorway to my room: they mirror each other across the threshold, propping up the doorframe, arms folded hard. There are squeaks from Mr Stanford's buttercup-yellow waterproofs. Rachel has draped a cardigan over the T-shirt which emphasizes the knot of her arms.

Mr Stanford creaks taller, ready to move away. 'Fresh air will help.'

Rachel bends fiercely into the fold of her arms: 'I *can't*, okay?' she bellows after him, even though he has moved no more than half an inch, has swayed rather than moved. 'I can't go clambering over rocks all day with a swollen endometrium.'

Endometrium is impressive; I wish that I could see Mr Stanford's appreciation. The tone of his reply, however, is studiously bland: 'I can't have you lounging around here all day. So I'll expect you to join us in five minutes.'

I am close to his shiny back, now, but he does not know that I am here, nor, apparently, does Rachel, because her eyes do not move from his face. Behind me, I can hear someone bumping through the door.

I try to appeal, 'Mr Stanford . . .'

But Rachel finishes, 'You're a *pathetic wanker*,' and flops away.

Mr Stanford swings deep into the room, silver eddies on his waterproofs, to yell, '*I'll have you for that, no one speaks like that to staff, you'll be in a lot of trouble when we go back to school.*'

'Oh yes?' her voice comes weary and muffled from the depths. 'And who'll believe you?'

His hands rise, then slap back onto the doorframe: dismay, then emphasis, 'Don't be ridiculous.' But I see the nervous flutter of his glue-yellow fingernails on the white-painted wood. '*In any case*,' he swells, 'I have *witnesses*.' And his face slides around to me.

I have to stand my ground, to tell him, 'I don't think that you do.'

So his eyes widen to latch onto Lawrence. I know that it is Lawrence who has come up behind me because I can hear him wheeze, the rhythmic twang of his bronchioles. I turn and see the splayed hands of the shrug with which he places himself beyond Mr Stanford's reach, *Sorry, mate, I heard nothing.* Three pairs of eyes bob behind Lawrence: Susie, Trina and Avril have arrived. Trina says, 'In fact, *none of us* is feeling too good, *all of us* are having our periods.'

Before I can laugh, Mr Stanford roars at us, '*Stop it,*' the command spurting from a faceful of loathing.

Suddenly Rachel is in the doorway again, hands high on the frame, tiny wings of cotton in her armpits. 'It happens,' she says to his back, and when he turns, her head inclines to one side, 'or didn't you know? Happens in girls' boarding schools and nunneries, or wherever women live together in close confines; we fall into sync, our hormones mix in the air or something.'

'True,' adds Trina, who would not have known; she knows very little biology.

Mr Stanford flings his reply around all of us, '*Of course* I know that,' but his puffing face is squashed by a frown.

Susie announces, 'Mine is so bad that I need to lie down,' and swishes on his waterproof on her way into our room. She trails her own waterproof, which whispers from the floor.

I cannot believe that this will work.

Mr Stanford's gaze hops around us, from face to face, sharp, looking for a weak link; but in the meantime, he tries to seem to move towards conciliation, 'Oh *come on,* girls.'

Rachel unwinds her mouth, but this is not quite a smile. 'Looks like you're five girls short of an expedition.'

He coughs up a laugh, forces himself one step further from conciliation to good humour. '*Girls,* don't be *silly.*'

'Oh, but *we are* silly, because of those silly hormones of ours,' Rachel lowers her head so far that it comes close to her shoulder, 'but of course, it's part of our charm.'

'Avril?' he asks, suddenly; he has decided that she is the weak link.

She shivers to attention. 'What?'

He bullies her, 'You can't tell me that you *and all your friends here* are indisposed?'

She manages a faint echo, 'Indisposed.' How much of this has she missed? Someone elbows her, and with a wobble she adds, 'Oh, yes, I'm always indisposed.'

Trina whoops, 'Never a truer word!'

Rachel folds down from the doorframe, slowly, calmly, and says to Mr Stanford, 'You're always telling us that the only truth is science, that truth is proof and proof is science. You're always telling us to believe nothing unless we have proof. Now you have a hypothesis, that we don't all have our periods today. So, where's your proof?'

Faced with this challenge, Mr Stanford stamps away down the corridor and slams the door. The sound wave crashes into our silence.

Trina whispers, 'Temper, temper,' and we scurry into our room.

Rachel is sitting on her bed with her pillow held hard to her stomach. Suddenly she is struck, '*Lawrence.*'

Trina echoes with, '*Loz.*'

We turn to see him drowning in the darkness of the corridor, flapping away our concern. 'It's okay, it's okay.'

I am horrified, 'It *is not* okay.' We overlooked him because everything happened so quickly.

Susie appeals to him, 'Come in here, for God's sake.'

Trina calls, 'You can say that you have prostate trouble.'
She seems serious.

He stops.

Rachel worries her lower lip with a sharp tooth. 'We could
try saying that we need you here to look after us.'

Avril wants to know, 'But what *is* wrong with us?'

Trina despairs, '*I'd* like to know what is wrong with
you.'

But suddenly we are knocked back into silence by the
thump of the far door.

Frozen, we listen to the approach of Mr Stanford's steps,
but they stop short of our doorway.

'Why don't you walk around down on the shore,' he says,
presumably to Lawrence, 'see what you can find in the rock
pools, do much the same as you did yesterday.' His voice is
low, is a display of kindness and a play for conspiracy: he is
wary of Lawrence, now, but has to try to win him over. The
implication of this plan for Lawrence is that he can go alone
to the shore, which means that he will not have to go, or not
for very long.

Suddenly there are two more steps and Mr Stanford looms
close to our doorway, but remains in the corridor, from where
he addresses us *en masse*: '*You lot* have a *bug*,' these words
spat and orchestrated by jabs of his index finger. And now
he is gone.

When the far door crashes, Rachel flops sideways onto her
bed and whines into her pillow, 'A *bug*, that's *pathetic*, *he's*
pathetic.'

'Look on the bright side,' I tell her, 'this could cause trouble
for those caterers.'

*   *   *

The end of Day Four, which is the end of the trip: Day Five requires us only to *Depart*.

We have had dinner and now we are in the library. This is our first visit to the library, which was discovered half an hour ago by Trina who had decided to wander around the building rather than face a dish of shepherd's pie, which she had nicknamed *sheep worrier's pie*. We stayed, but as we trooped from the canteen, she called to us from the top of a short flight of stairs. When we reached her, she enthused, 'Get a load of this!' then lunged to open one of the doors with a fanfare, 'Da *da*!'

We hurried inside to claim one of the long tables and six of the chairs which are almost armchairs. No one else came in here after dinner, and now the old stone building holds a deep hush crumpled only slightly and rarely by cymbals in the kitchens below. We are sprawled, heads on arms, our talk sliding over the shiny surface. The table is warmed by an avenue of lamps with jade shades. The wax is cooking, smells to me like a mixture of butter and honey. Which mixes in turn with the trace of soap dried into the crook of my arm. I feel warm and clean for the first time in five days. The wood of this table could have been made from chestnuts hammered smooth; occasionally I feel that I am slipping on the surface, even though I am as low as I can go. From here, the rain sounds dry, like the hiss of seeds in a shaken pod, and looks wonderful, the luminous streamers and their stray raindrops clean and intricately linked on our black windows.

Yesterday we had our day off, but today we had to work much harder than usual. Jim and Mr Stanford goaded us, yelling through the fizzy spray for us to *Take it easy* but ensuring that this was impossible. They chose a particularly steep and exposed stretch of shore for the belated barnacle head count. Then we were allowed twenty minutes for lunch, rather than forty: *Lots to do.* And at the end of the day we were not allowed to leave the shore until three quarters of an hour later than usual.

Our day off had been like a Sunday but better, with gossip and tapes, face packs and make-up. Lawrence had dawdled on the beach for a while, luminous in his waterproofs, shrunk to a toddler far below our window. We saw him throwing sticks and stones across the water. No one else ventured from our room, until we had to go to dinner because we had finished our own supplies. In the canteen, Mr Stanford had tittered, 'Hello, girls, are you better?' as if there was a joke which he was in on. Then he said nothing more to us until he came to our main door unnecessarily early this morning, sometime before seven o'clock, to scream, '*Wakey wakey, wakey wakey!*'

I sparked awake to see Rachel, to see her wake. Her face lagged behind her, filled with sleep. Disgusted, she muttered, 'Wanky wanky, in his case.'

Now, in the library, the muscles in my back and legs are hot and heavy from the long, hard day. For the last half an hour, we have talked of nothing else but the injustice of this week, our exile to this peninsula, this enforced biology. All of us except Lawrence, but his eyes follow the conversation, rippling his sagged brow like a dog's. One of us is kicking a table leg, has been doing so for quite a while; a slack kick, but these aimless prods have been knocking through our tender bones and building up in our bloodstream. Slumped here, in one another's warmth, our faces are droopy and darkening.

'We've lost a week of our lives,' Rachel moans into the blurred reflection of her lips.

'I wish that we *had* lost it,' Susie sighs through a stray strand of hair. 'It's been the *worst* week of *my* life.'

'Worst *and* utterly pointless,' I remind her.

Trina snarls, 'This place should be burned down. With Jim inside.'

'*And* Mr Stanford,' adds Rachel.

'Well *of course* Mr Stanford.'

Rachel hauls her eyes to Trina's face, then smiles. 'He's the kindling.'

Trina looks worried, 'Sounds too nice, for him,' and turns on one of her pockets. 'We *could* burn it down,' she chucks the box of matches high above us, the little yellow and black box a big square bee which drops dead into the palm of her hand. All the matches click simultaneously on the bottom of the box. It is hard to know if she is serious.

Avril chips in, 'Or at least smash it up a bit.'

I see four heads jerk, and in the corner of my eye I detect one smile, Lawrence's smile, so secret that even he lowers his own eyes.

Rachel laughs, 'Well, don't let us stop you, Av, if you feel so strongly,' but suddenly she is serious: 'I do think that we should do something; I do think that something should be done.' She stops to look around us, to check that she is speaking for all of us.

I have to point out, '*Not* something that will put us in a similar correctional institution, but for a lot longer than a week.'

She slots her hair down behind her ears, a decisive movement, the opposite of a shrug, to imply that she had already thought of this; and pointedly says nothing, *Goes without saying*.

I stand up and take a few paces to stretch my legs, to uncoil the blood that is sunk deep in them. The blood moves so slowly that it feels granular. I stroll down a wall of books. The spines are slotted so tightly together that I cannot imagine how any of them are ever taken away from the others. Many of them are ringed with combinations of various leathers, coloured from yellow to mahogany, and finished with a chain of gold letters. But, oddly, I am drawn to the pamphlets which are placed here and there in the impressive display. Their spines are too thin for the labels of their catalogue numbers, which are wrapped around regardless like tatty and useless plasters. I start with one of these pamphlets, reach and hook a finger over the top of one of the furry cardboard spines and beckon it down to me. It falls easily from two swollen hoary spines and drops into my hands like a dead butterfly. I walk across the room, the blood purring now in my calves, and push my pamphlet between two bulky books.

As I turn around, Susie stands so abruptly that it is as if a line has been cut and she has bobbed to the surface. Her walk, though, is purposeful. I am not sure that I have ever seen her like this, and certainly not this week, when her only freely-chosen movement has been her stumble down the corridor to the phone. Now she selects a big book, the weight of which seems to surprise her, but to which she rises. She carries this book in a firm fold of arms which is further clamped by a frown of concentration. On the other side of the room, she swaps the book for another, which she swaps for yet another to cover her tracks.

With Trina, it is different. She stands with a slap of the

table, skips to the wall to snatch a slimmer book which she moves to the shelf below, and runs with the newly-displaced volume to other shelves where she shuffles books. Whenever she pushes a book into place, she delivers an extra slap to the spine. Rachel has been watching us, levered high on her arms: her gaze scans us and in a few seconds she has seen the implications. Suddenly she is up, and busy with books. She zigzags the room more than we do, seems to cut deeper into the order of the shelves. Avril moves one pamphlet, but when she returns to her chair, her face is transformed, full and vivid with a smile. Lawrence pauses to decide where to put his book but in the end fails to manage anything worse than a clean swap, which is better than nothing.

After a minute or two, we clunk back into our chairs, on to our table. The library is no longer fully functional, but looks no different from before, remains beautiful. The damage is invisible, and beyond repair. There are too few misplaced books to raise suspicion: if a book is missing from its place on the shelf, then it is on loan, or it is a unique loss; if a book is found in an inappropriate place, then this is a simple mistake, a small carelessness. No one will ever know what we have done. The return of books to their proper places will be haphazard and piecemeal. Eventually some books will wash up, but never all of them; some will stay sunk on these shelves forever.

3

TIE-BREAKER

I kick open the kitchen door, my hands full of my colouring book and pens.

Inside, Mum is telling Dad, 'She should have a proper meal.'

I slide onto a chair, sit up at the table.

Mum says to me, 'Can't you go in there?' and her head jerks towards the door, the living-room.

'I need a surface.'

Noisily clearing too much space for my book and pens, she continues, 'I don't want her to go back again without having had some proper food.'

She means Alison.

'Well,' Dad says cheerily to his newspaper, 'she said she'd have salad.'

'But when she says salad, she means salad *cream*. She pushes the salad around her plate then mops up the salad cream with bread; haven't you seen her do that?'

'Her grandmother is a greengrocer, remember; I'm sure that she has plenty of greens.'

'Her *grandmother* works too hard, her *grandmother* is too old and tired to play *mum*. I wouldn't be surprised if the last thing that she wants to see at the end of the day is a green; I wouldn't blame her if she nips two doors down to Giuseppe for chips.'

Whenever Mum takes us into the shop, Alison's grandma

gives each of us an apple: this means three apples now that Michaela has teeth. Eliza and I say *Thanks-Mrs-Mortimer*, Michaela's version is *Ta-Mi-Moma*. None of us are keen on apples, but we pretend. Mum tells Dad that the apples are embarrassing, that they make us look like scroungers; but when he says that she can always go somewhere else, her answer is *I've shopped there since the day I was married and I suppose I'll shop there until the day I drop.*

Dad says, 'I think that Mrs Mortimer and Tim are coping very well.'

Mum's hands are propped on her hips, they look like claws. '*Coping*. They'll need to do more than *cope*. You think she's coming back, don't you. You're a fool, like Tim.'

Uncle Tim, Alison's dad, has a gold tooth in the corner of his smile. I love that tooth, it must have a story to it, like a locket or a scar. Mum says, *That tooth always surprises me, you'd never think that he was the type.* I could try a gold tooth for the face I am drawing in my book; but of the pens that I have, the closest to gold is yellow. And yellow is not quite the same. A yellow tooth would be quite different.

Across the table from me, Dad warns, 'Shhh,' and cocks his head towards the door.

'Oh, *she* knows,' Mum says. 'It's you men who won't believe that her mother has abandoned you.'

Another, 'Shhh,' but this nod is for me.

'Oh, Madam's oblivious when she's drawing.'

I hardly even remember what Alison's mum looked like; she went away so long ago. She was not around for Christmas last year, or even the summer holidays. Of course I remember her hair, the colour of her hair: close to the colour of Uncle Tim's tooth. *One of the tricks of the trade*, was Mum's joke, because Auntie Anne had been a hairdresser. Perhaps she *is* a hairdresser, in her new life – Mum told me that she has a new life. She was supposed to have given up when she married Uncle Tim but she never quite did, because sometimes we were put on a high stool in the middle of her kitchen so that she could trim our hair. When she was trimming my hair, I could smell her perfume, handcream, and washing powder, I would close my eyes and listen to her special scissors, her sleeve on her arm, her high heels whenever she took one of her definite steps to one side or the other. Sometimes a cold blade would brush my forehead, the tip of my ear. Feathers of hair would fall and settle on my shoulders, then eventually topple and fall onto the tiles in a circle around me. My fallen hair was darker than Eliza's: we dropped trails of hair that did not mix. And then, not wanting to leave her out, Auntie Anne would graze Michaela's baby fluff with her blades.

Dad leans harder over his newspaper but says sideways to Mum, 'You worry too much, Alison's hardly tubby.'

'Oh, I *know* that; that's my *point*: she's a scrap, she's looking poorly.' Mum has come to the table and picked up my black pen, she is tapping the tabletop with the white lidded tip.

Dad says, 'She's missing her mum.'

'Aren't we all, but we have to keep going.' The pen returns to the others, is slotted into line.

'Her brother seems better.'

'Oh, *that* bruiser. I'm glad we never had a boy.'

'But, he's older, he has friends.'

And today he is with those friends, playing football somewhere, leaving us in peace. The boy in my picture is wearing shorts which are too long to be football shorts. His knees are chubby, like the girl's cheeks; I am going to have to use a lot of pink.

When Mum went to have Michaela in hospital, Eliza and I had to stay with Auntie Anne whenever Dad was at work. Just like Alison and Jason, now, staying sometimes with Mrs Mortimer. Mum had problems with Michaela, she was in hospital for weeks before Michaela was born. So for weeks I stayed in Auntie Anne's kitchen while she cooked, washed up, tidied, ironed. And this was what I wanted: I did not want her to worry over me, I wanted to colour in the pictures in my books while she hummed and turned between the sink, the cooker, the cupboards. I wondered about Mum: where she was, what she was doing, and what if she never came back. While I was colouring, I liked to listen to Eliza playing with Jason and Alison in the garden, their laughs sliding into the kitchen on the sunshine, over the blue and white tiles. I liked to hear Auntie Anne's laugh, too, when she was on the phone in the hallway: there was something in this laugh of hers which told me that she had forgotten that I was there.

During the summer, I moved from the kitchen down the hallway to the living-room, to try to draw some of Uncle Tim's tropical fish: *drawing from life*, Auntie Anne called this. I drew and coloured a whole book of fish. The day when Mum came to fetch us, she took brand new Michaela into the kitchen and stayed for a while. I could hear her laughing and complaining that Michaela had been born early, a few weeks before Auntie Anne's birthday, because otherwise they could have shared the same birthday. Whenever I looked up, I could see her and Auntie Anne through the serving hatch. They were both sitting on those high stools. Auntie Anne's legs were crossed, but so closely that her bare feet were side by side on the same rung; her legs looked like a long silvery tail. I called through to ask Auntie Anne how old she was going to be. Her quick laugh could have been a cough. 'Rox!'

Mum said, 'Twenty-one,' and smiled without moving her mouth.

Then Auntie Anne told the truth: 'Twenty-one years older than you, I'm going to be twenty-seven.'

'I'm six.' I was thinking aloud, although not very loudly.

'I know you are,' she said, more quietly.

And now I am eight. Like Alison. Alison and I are the same. Our mums were the same, too.

Now Mum leans back on the twin-tub and complains about Alison: 'What's she doing in there? She watches too much telly. And much too close to the screen. Kids – why do they do that? What do they think they're going to miss?' Her voice sweeps towards me. 'Why do you kids do that?'

I look up at her as I have been told to do when she talks to me, but I keep my pen moving and, below me, blue felt-tip is turning a piece of my picture into water.

And she is already telling Dad, 'I'll call her in here to *choose* what she wants for her salad, then perhaps we won't have to suffer that painful pushing of stuff around her plate.'

But Dad says, 'I don't think she's watching telly, I think she's listening for the phone.'

And I know why.

'Phone? Why? Who's ringing her? I *told* Mrs Mortimer that I'd take her home, around seven. In fact, I told her *twice*, because I know that she never listens; and, yes, I do know that she tries hard, but the fact is that she *never listens*.'

Dad says, 'She thinks there'll be a call for her when they've drawn the raffle.'

'You bought her a ticket? And she thinks she's going to *win*?' Mum's eyes look harder than normal.

'That's why you enter a raffle, isn't it? To win?'

'That's why *you* enter a raffle, perhaps. That's why *dreamers* enter raffles.' A quick, deep breath. '*Why* did you buy her a ticket? You know what she's like, you know what she was like with the Win-a-Pony competition. Why did you raise her hopes like this?'

'There's no harm in hoping.' Dad frowns over his newspaper.

'There's *every* harm in hoping,' Mum continues to the top of his head, 'because she's going to *lose*, and don't you think that she's had to face enough disappointments?'

Dad dares to peek up at her. 'Perhaps she *will* win.'

But Mum folds her arms and crashes them on to her tummy. '*Reality* is where *you* keep a *holiday home*: one ticket? Swilling around in that bin with all those hundreds?'

'*Five* tickets,' I have to tell her. Alison stands a much better chance than us because Dad bought a whole book of tickets for her, but the usual one ticket each for Eliza and me, and none for Michaela because she is too young and, anyway, she was on the other side of the field with Mum. Every year, the prize is the same, and every year this day is more important to me than Christmas, but I know that we have to be nice to Alison because her mum has a new life.

'*Five tickets?*' Mum's eyes flash the ceiling, several flashes, as if she is searching for more words.

Dad gives up on his paper, huffs back in his chair. 'Alison's in bad need of some fun.'

'And *I'm* in bad need of some *housekeeping*. Whatever made you think that we could afford *five tickets*?'

'Oh come on, Gina, this was a one-off.'

'A one-off here, a one-off there. Are we going to be doing these endless one-offs for the next ten years? The kid needs bringing up, not showering with presents.'

Dad's hands open in front of him. '*Five little raffle tickets* –'

'We have to put this behind us, now; we have to continue our lives as normal.' But suddenly she has turned away, and mutters to the window, 'Six months and no word from her mother.'

Quietly, Dad answers back, 'She *has* written to Mrs M.'

'Yes, and what exactly did she tell poor old Mrs Mortimer?' Turning around, Mum's face is as white as the sunny window. 'That she has *gone away to think*.' Now she is near to Dad, leaning over him, and I hear the rattle of her earrings in her hair. '*Think*.'

Now her eyes switch to mine. '*What's up?*'

This has made me jump: nothing is *up*.

She bashes her hair behind one ear. 'You're not going to make a fuss about *salad*, are you? Because I'm not in the mood for one of your fusses.'

Have I *ever* made a fuss about salad? Tomato is my fourth favourite food, cucumber my sixth. But as she has asked, I decided to try my luck: 'No lettuce?'

'No lettuce,' this is amazingly quick, but she adds, 'although I don't know *why*, because don't you *want* healthy bones?'

What would unhealthy bones be like? Do I have them already? Would I know if I had them?

Her eyes have turned back to Dad. 'Perhaps we should talk

to Tim about a pet for Alison. Surely he could manage a cat.'

'I did talk to Tim.'

'You did?'

'And he says that she isn't interested.'

'In a cat?'

Mum always says that *Animals are trouble, but cats are the best of a bad bunch.*

'In anything.'

She takes several steps nowhere in particular, but bumps into the corner of the table, rattling my row of pens. 'But these competitions! That ridiculous business of the Win-a-Pony, and now this!'

'I know, I know,' Dad's hands rise but stay, hovering an inch above the tabletop, 'but she seems to want to *win* one.'

'But that's *silly*,' Mum hisses. 'Why do kids do this? Why do they have to be so *impossible* about everything?'

His hands are back on the table. 'This seems to be something that she wants to do on her own.'

'Well, *fine*: she could save up. She has pocket money, you know; Roxanne tells me that she has two shillings every week from Tim, and Mrs Mortimer seems to slip her more than the odd sixpence. Isn't that right, Rox?'

I look up from the blank bucket which I have topped with blue water, look from Mum to Dad, and nod. And now will Dad realize that I am badly off for pocket money, compared to everyone else?

He looks but does not seem to see me. He tells Mum, 'Tim says that she's more than happy to save for the food and everything, she *has* saved, but she refuses to spend this money on *buying* the animal: she wants to *win* one.'

'Well, this is silly.' Mum joins us, drops into a chair, drops her elbows onto the table and her chin into her hands.

The corners of Dad's mouth fold in and down, they press dimples into his cheeks.

I wish that I could draw dimples, but whenever I try, they look like boils.

He says, 'She wants to be lucky, I suppose.'

'Well, I'm afraid that I hope that she's unlucky with this one. Because what would she do with a racing greyhound?'

I put down my pen. I have to explain this to Mum every year on the day of the kennel fête: 'You don't have to *do anything* with the greyhound, Mum. If you win him, then you're his owner, you make up his name, you can go and see him whenever you want, but he lives in the kennels and they feed him, train him, race him.' The ideal dog, surely, in her opinion. The only dog, I suspect, that she would ever allow us to have. Because she says that *They're worse than kids; they're always under your feet or mating with your leg; they're noisy and smelly and they have to be taken everywhere; they eat that foul food and they poo everywhere.*

Dad says they do not poo everywhere if they have been trained. And he knows, because his family had lots of them when he was little. He seems to remember them by how they died: Bruno as a puppy from a virus, Jake in old age from diabetes, Slipper by mistake from rat poison.

Across the table, Mum shuts her eyes hard, then opens them hard: a sign that she refuses to say a word.

Once, I pointed out to her that Grandma's poodle, Rebel, has never mated with our legs, but she said, 'That yapping perm is incapable of mating with *anything*.'

And so we have Leo: for my fifth birthday, I was allowed to choose from the box of kittens and I chose him because he looked sad and trodden on, but this is how he has behaved ever since, he has never grown happy or clever. We hardly ever see him: the only evidence that he lives here is his two bowls on our kitchen floor.

One of Mum's arms flops down onto the table; her head stays in her other hand. 'But how on earth would Tim find the time to keep running Alison up to the kennels? He's forever ferrying her from home to school to Mrs Mortimer.'

'She was *fine* when she failed to win that pony,' Dad sounds worried. 'She seemed to accept the situation.'

'And how do *you* know?' Mum squeaks. Her other arm thuds onto the table. The thud jogs me, jogs my pen so that the red bucket seems to have grown an extra handle. 'When are *you* ever here to see how she is? You men, off to work every day. Who stays around to pick up the pieces? What else was she going to do, other than *accept the situation*? But how do *any* of us know what she was going through? That obsession, those books ... she was coming here with what must have been the library's entire collection of books on ponies. And then she spent her birthday money on more pony books. All for four or five questions, four or five little questions on that entry form. And she was ringing up local farmers, you know; did you know that? Asking questions. About feeding and forelocks and whatever. Mrs Mortimer found her on the phone, a couple of times, asking questions about hooves and hay, whatever. And that notebook full of tie-breakers! She was working on her tie-breaker for months, lots of clever little lines.' Mum has to stop for breath. 'Apparently she'd always wanted a pony, but never this badly. And do you know what she said to me when she knew that she hadn't won? *There's always next year*. Just like that: *There's always next year*. Sometimes, I have to say, she gives me the creeps.'

'Gina, please,' Dad whispers, his head turning towards the door.

I keep all my wishes for a pony; I wish on every first star that I see, on every birthday candle that I blow. And I tell no one, because if I told, those wishes would be wiped away. I have had so many wishes by now that eventually one of them will come true. But in the meantime I would love to win the greyhound.

'She's so like Tim, in some ways; wouldn't you say?' Mum is quieter, now. 'Sitting by the phone, but firm in her belief that there's-always-next-year. And in other ways she's the opposite: so much hope and determination. Tim could do with some of that; we might have had Anne back by now if he had made an effort to find her, if he had gone after her.'

Should I chance this red pen on the girl's cheeks? Does anyone really have red cheeks? Even someone with cheeks as chunky as these?

'But you said that we should let her go.'

'Yes, *now*. But if Tim had had more get up and go, she might never have got up and gone.'

How did she go? On a bus?

'That's unfair.' Dad sounds tired. 'Tim's a lovely bloke.'

'I *know* he's a lovely bloke.' Mum, too: very tired. 'Perhaps that was the problem.'

'What do you mean?'

I know a good word for this girl: *apple-cheeked*. The apples that we are given by Mrs Mortimer have red on them, she has to find the three most beautiful apples in the box. Mum walks around behind her, saying, *Anything will do, really, honestly*; but Mrs Mortimer laughs and says, *No, no, looks are important.*

'Well, you know, not everyone wants *a lovely bloke*, or not all the time.'

'They don't?'

Mum breathes down her nose. 'You wouldn't understand. This place . . .'

'There are worse places.' Dad seems to be checking through his newspaper for something; the turning pages fan me, fluffing my hair.

'Well, yes, of course, but what are the two main excitements, here, every year?' Mum leaves us and crosses to the window. 'The kennel fête,' she says to the window, 'and the point-to-point: fund-raising for greyhounds, and betting on horses.'

I love the point-to-point, I love to walk over the fields which are usually only a boring view from our bedroom windows, fields which look flat from our bedroom windows but which, when we walk on them, are clumps of grass. I love to walk to the hedges that have been built for the horses to jump: higher than real hedges, impossibly high. Then there are the marquees, massive, with tatty flaps for doorways. Everyone from around here comes to the races, but there are hundreds of other people and I have no idea where they come from. Nor do I have any idea where the horses and jockeys come from; but they are proper horses and jockeys, they look like the horses and jockeys that I have seen on the telly. Lots of people have picnics: paper plates and sausage rolls.

'You *met me* at the point-to-point.' Dad closes the paper, squashes those crackles into silence.

Mum laughs, but not much; just two low, slow notes. 'I

met lots of boys at the point-to-point; there's a beer tent, there are lots of boys. Lots of horrible, drunken boys.'

If she had married one of those other boys, would I have been born? Would I have been *me*?

'Don't talk about our fathers like that.' Dad's laugh is quicker, thrown higher.

'*Anne's* father had drunk himself six feet under by the time we were old enough to go to the point-to-point on our own.'

Six feet under means dead: a *Mr* Mortimer, dead. Why had I never thought that there would have been a *Mr* Mortimer?

'You know what Anne and I loved about the point-to-point? The refreshments tent.'

Me, too: the smell of cake.

'The cream teas, coffee kisses; we had a passion for those coffee kisses.'

'Sugar and spice.'

'Sugar and spice,' but now she sounds far away, further away than the window. 'Beer and bets. Anyway, why did you say that you met me there? We'd known each other since we were five, since Mrs Goodchild's class.'

'I *spoke properly* to you for the first time at a point-to-point.' Dad has joined her by the window.

A moment of silence. '*Im*properly.'

'I don't think that I'd have spoken improperly to you, I don't think that I'd have known how to do that.'

'Yes, but you know what I mean.' She is turning her wedding ring, her only ring; a spark of sunshine stays in place, on top. 'Remember how drunk Tim was?'

'Our Timbo? Our Timmy, horrible and drunk?'

'Well, horribly drunk.'

'Horribly *sick*.'

Suddenly she takes his face into her hands. 'You showed me your teeth.'

He looks surprised, his hands on her shoulders. 'Sounds rather aggressive.'

'No, you showed me your two chipped teeth.' She slips the tip of her nail between his lips. 'You and Tim had come off your motorbike, the day before. Remember?'

Dad had a motorbike?

His hands drop on to her hips. 'I remember coming off the bike, I remember the teeth, but I don't remember that I showed them to you.'

'Well, you did,' she says up into his eyes.

'Well, I'm sorry,' he says down into hers.

Stroking his hair, her ring disappears in the shiny darkness. 'I was touched.'

'By the chips in my teeth?' He is laughing, trying to suck his lips over his teeth.

I am laughing inside, picturing potato chips held in his teeth.

And Mum laughs in a way that I had forgotten that she could laugh. 'The chink in your armour, I suppose.'

Armour?

'Not touched enough to come to the pictures with me. Or not *straight away.*'

And Mum loves the pictures; she has promised to take me to see her favourite film, *Gone With the Wind*, whenever it comes again to our cinema.

'So, why did you change your mind a week or so later?'

'Because of Anne.'

'Because of *Anne?*'

'I never told you? Well, Tim seemed so keen on her, and

I knew that he was a nice boy; and she'd had such a rough year, with her dad dying. And, of course, she didn't want to know, when Tim was throwing up around the beer tent; but I thought that if we met up again as a foursome, then I could probably persuade her that he was okay.' She smiles, 'And I did,' the smile becomes smaller, 'I suppose.'

I look back down, but my picture means nothing to me: I have finished, filled the blank spaces with colours, but there is nothing more than a girl and a boy carrying a bucket down a hillside. I have had enough, for today: when I have packed up these pens, I am going next door to try to be friendly to Alison.

As I open the door, Dad asks Mum, 'Do you really think that she has gone off with someone else?'

And as I close the door behind me, I hear Mum's whisper: 'Listen, remember when I came home from the hospital, and I went to fetch the kids? Well, Rox came running to open the door, she'd been in the front room; but Anne was in the kitchen, and as I walked into the hallway, I'm fairly sure that I saw someone leaving by the back door.'

4

NIGHT FLIGHT

'No kids?' she asks me, with a laugh of exasperation as she kneels to her toddler who has ended up near my table in his tantrum.

'Not yet.' My standard reply.

'Married, then?'

'Yes.' Technically, no; but yes is easier, yes will do.

'Not here with you, though?'

All week I have been mesmerized not by her bulk, but by the suntan-coloured hair which licks down her back and around her waist. Now, from above, I see the lips of the parting around a rosy sliver of scalp. She stands, and the child turns to her.

I wrinkle my nose, 'No time off work.' True. 'But I needed a break.'

'Been here before?' She picks up and cuddles the boy; his whine whipped away like waves wrapped into a seashell.

'Yes,' and for some reason, I laugh apologetically, 'once. You?'

'No,' but a similar laugh, 'never been abroad before. Had a tiny windfall and decided to blow it on some winter sun.'

'Wise choice.'

Her smile stretches to match mine and now she is on her way back to the beach, her son shrunk to a kitten in her arms, her wide hips rocking a low hem.

*   *   *

We have been neighbours for a week until this morning, when we vacated our semi-detached, identically furnished villas. But this is the first time that we have spoken. Sometimes we swapped smiles, but only when the man was elsewhere – she would smile only when he was elsewhere. He never acknowledged me, not even on our twinned patios through the bush of bougainvillaea that was our border. His face was made of orange peel, his legs were porcelain but over-fired and cracked by hairs; his glasses magnified the sun and boiled his eyes in their own water. He used their patio as a platform from where he could bellow to the little boy. The child was prone to tantrums; I learned to dread the petulant quiver of his knees.

I never saw them talk to anyone. Apart from the yells of the man and the child, the only exchanges that I overheard were muffled by their whitewashed walls and diluted by the drizzle of their satellite television. There is not much to do here, but I had no time to try my television. Every day I followed the sun around my patio: always on the move, the sun, my towel, my books and me. Then there were meals: the strenuous chewing of fresh loaves, the languid peeling of fruits. Plus snacks, the crunching of crisps succulent with heavy Spanish oil, the snapping of the dry folded wings from cricket-green pistachios. Then numerous trips to the little shops to replenish supplies. And a daily clean and tidy in preparation for the maid, who came to slosh the floors and bathroom with lemon-sweetened bleach. More strolls and coffees. Often I was late to leave the esplanade, nearly too late for a last trip to the shops.

This island is an ideal place from where to watch the world go by; or, rather, the people of the world, overhead in planes.

Flat on my back on my towel, I would watch those planes, which were too high to be landing here or on any of the neighbouring islands. Bound for elsewhere. For anywhere and everywhere other than here. Down here on the ground, there is very little to see. Sparse vegetation on volcanic mountains. The population is small, and the number of tourists limited. Traffic is taxis, which are old red Mercedes with leathery upholstery; or tourists' hire-cars, very new, very white, very small, like toy cars on these toytown roads. Last year, we drove to the capital, desperate for some life. On the main waterfront we went into a bar which was empty except for a group of girls, girls of nine or ten who were wearing white blouses and pleated skirts and who ordered meals which were served graciously by their rather formally-dressed waiter. Outside, in the road, there were other, similar girls, with skipping-ropes, their arms looped around one another's shoulders.

This year, I came here alone for the peace and quiet: the inky sea, the eye-blue sky and, of course, the sun. And there is the moon, which, this week, was full. The moon was the reason why I did not mind when the neighbours' son soared like a seagull from sleep in the early mornings: because, waking early, I woke to moonshine. The moon, here, seesaws slowly with the heavy sun. Every morning I woke to a moonshine stencil of my window draped Dali-esque over my bed. By nine, my neighbours had gone for the day. Why did they go, every day, all day, when there was a pool and playground in the garden? The beach, I suppose. From my patio, I would see the man unfold the pushchair and pack a bucket and spade. Once, later, I saw them in a café with cooked breakfasts: chips, bacon, eggs, and fried sliced white bread. The woman saw me looking, and swallowed hard on nothing. Her gaze clunked on to her plate and bounced away to catch the ferry which slides all day between here and Fuerteventura but never slides from view. What did she think that she saw in my eyes? Disapproval, even disgust? A fat woman guzzling fatty food? I burned to tell her what I had seen before she saw me: her velvet brown hair dropped down and around her solid gold shoulders; the lightness of her eyes and corners of her mouth.

Whenever I came back from town for the evening they were already home, patio door shut, curtains drawn. And it was for this, and only this, that I pitied the woman: she never went into the garden in darkness. No one else stayed around, in the evenings; everyone went into town, which I did not do because I did not want to walk alone on unlit roads. I watched them leave, each family buzzing around their one torch. Later, the only sound was the clatter of palm leaves, which, initially, I mistook for the splatter of water on hard soil. I would go on the trail of honeysuckle, slowly circling bushes to coax the scent. Sometimes I had to wait for the creamy moon to be drawn up through a steam of cloud. Then everything in this dry land was slippery with moonshine: the flat roofs, the red rocks, the ruffled Atlantic.

This morning, earlier than necessary, my neighbours shepherded their suitcases through the garden to the luggage store. When the maid came, she pushed a cot from their villa onto their patio, to air. Metal cage and wipe-down mattress. The bars were ablaze in the sunshine, but later, when I heard the wheels follow her away, I was shivering.

I had seen the man's suspicion that there was something

wrong with my mind or my life: because why else come here alone? Or – *and* – my life was too good for my own good, nothing but bikinis and books. I could see that this was closer to *her* opinion: in her eyes, I was slim and leisurely. But they were wrong. I am here to gather strength for an operation. It is the surgeon who needs the strength, though: there is no other way to a heart than to saw through the breastbone.

In a routine check, three years ago, my blood pressure gave me away: too high one moment, too low the next. So the doctor listened to my heart and heard the murmur. I cannot separate *murmur* from *discontent*: a murmur of discontent in the white clench of my ribs. A complaint to which I would have remained deaf. I had been so sure that I would know if I was ill, I would have symptoms, pains and lumps. It was odd to have to be informed of a failure of my own body. The doctor has explained about the backwash of blood, that she can hear the whoosh of blood up and away into my body and then a sigh as a little drops back down into my heart through the leaky valve. I am bleeding into my own heart. A heart which has to work harder and harder to send enough blood around my body, and will become strained and sunk in pooled blood: *Weak and flabby* were the doctor's words for my heart.

I had been brought up to dread cancer, busy and messy. Not this trickle to death, not this tiny mechanical defect. For thirty-three years I have lived with this leaky valve of mine; for three years I have been monitored, and now my doctor says that it is time for a small repair. As simple as that, as far as she is concerned. But I can only think that, in the time before such operations, I would have died of this one tiny imperfection. And when I think of all the hearts in the world, and of all the hearts that there have ever been, I am amazed that almost every valve will fit and stay watertight. Blood-tight. I am amazed that so many bodies are so perfect.

Technically, I am dying: without an operation, I will die, but not for years. But with the operation I will die as soon as I am opened, because the surgeons will disconnect my defective heart and divert my life through machines. My doctor says that when they are happy with their stitch-in-time, they will turn my blood back to me, and I will thaw and live again. I am not quite sure that I believe her. Recently I asked her, 'Can I leave this leak?' She laughed as she said, '*Oh* no,' meaning, *Not if you want to stay alive.* Which was not what I asked her. Lately I have not been quite sure what I want. Except a holiday: I knew that it was time for a holiday. I came here, on holiday, to think everything through, which, so far, I have failed to do. Often I ponder the reassurances of my doctor: 'With a new valve you'll be as right as rain.' When I asked her if I could continue to delay, she was stern: 'You need to have this operation before you can get on with your life.' I think that she might have meant *children*. I am not sure what I think about children. I have found it impossible to think of babies with this heavy heart of mine.

When I vacated my villa, this morning, I stayed in the garden for a while. Through a bush I could see a child on a seesaw, but only the one child, only half of the fun. And those solitary rises and falls seemed too slow, to be in slow motion. Then, with the whole day to kill, I went for a stroll. All week I had stayed away from the beach because of the colonies of toddlers, the swell of their screams. But today, hot and homeless, I perched on a rock by the shore. Below, a baby was discovering sand; a German baby, whose mother's words of enthusiasm clattered on my ears, but whose face told me that this was special even in a life in which so much is new. Sand swirled around his tiny fingers until his mother carried him away to the water. I stepped from my rock, then lay down. How many years since I had been on, in, sand? I was stunned by the warmth and smoothness, which I did not remember from childhood, this must have been unimportant when I was a child. When I am home, I will come across this sand for weeks: in my bag, my books, my shoes. I love to think that this island will travel home with me, even on my body, gritting my toes and making golden candyfloss of the hairs on my arms.

At the end of the day, coming up from the beach, I made my way here for coffee and to watch the sun melt on to the horizon. My neighbour came and went: even though we have hours until our flight, without our villas we are already returned to our separate lives. I am turning cold. The air is thin with the clean chill of water; because it is winter, even here. I have watched the holiday-makers drain from the beach in this faint wash of dusk, but now in the distance some people are arriving: no, *children*, a small group of them, their busy feet skimming the tidal froth and stirring the custardy sand. Dark children whom I have never seen before. They are under the supervision of a man, but barely, because they kick flurries and only when I see the tracks do I realize that there is a pattern to this, that this is a team session, a training session. It is not these tracks that impress me, however, but the laughter: the smiles rise familiar in my eyes, like a memory; but new, too, as a possibility. Propelling themselves over the shadowed sand, they take me with them: somehow these low-flying children in a blood-orange sky have put a topspin on my heart.

POSSIBILITY OF
ELECTRICITY

For Pat Ashton

I remember Dad reading aloud the advert for the *finca*, I remember that when he quoted, 'Possibility of electricity', Mum looked up from the small plastic bowl of Sebastian's baby food and warned, '*No*, Mike.'

He peeped around the newspaper and laughed, 'You *don't want* electricity, Mags?'

Her tongue clicked on her sip of the baby's Banana Surprise, the temperature of which she was checking.

Dad's eyes switched emptily to the ceiling, then back behind the paper, as he reminded her, 'Good God, woman, I *am* an electrician.'

But the electrics turned out to be different in Spain, in an old *finca* on a high terrace of olive trees, and, anyway, he was not there when we needed him. His plan was that the *finca* would provide cheap holidays in the long-term for his family of five children, but for now he could spare no more than a week away from work because of the necessary loans. Anyway, the problem was sometimes more serious than he could have solved: during our first holiday, at Easter, the whole village was without power for days. During our second holiday, in the summer, our own supply showered suddenly from our shiny new sockets. When we were safely back home, and Mum was complaining to Dad, he could only remind her that he could not always come away with us because he had to work to fund these holidays of ours.

She shrieked, 'But I don't want *these* holidays, these aren't *holidays*, our *lives* are in *danger*.'

All that he could do was wail, 'But I've bought you a *finca*, a lovely *finca*.'

She replied, 'It's not lovely.'

He said, 'The *view* is lovely.'

She said, 'But we don't live in the *view*. I don't do my washing in the *view*.'

Whenever she tried to explain that she would rather have no holiday than stay alone in the *finca*, he would protest, 'You're *not* alone, you have the *kids*.'

Her lips would tighten but she would manage to say, 'Exactly.'

Like an accusation, he would say, 'You have Renee.'

Me: I was twelve; I had had my first period in the *finca* and been unable to flush away my sanitary towels because of the cesspit, and I had been unable to visit the local pool for almost a whole week.

He would laugh and call to me, '*Don't walk away . . . eh?*'

And Mum would shout at him, 'Oh *stop*, will you? Just shows how little you know: *walk away*? She never leaves her lilo.'

This was his cue to turn on me and shout, 'You should help your mother more, Renee.'

But Mum was beyond help, in Spain. This was not the Spain of her dreams, of cheerful, flamenco-dancing peasantry. This was Franco's Spain. There was a policeman who was always on duty in the village, in the middle of the Plaza, with a gun. My mother had two comments for him, never said to his face but muttered like charms whenever we trooped across the Plaza under his mirrored gaze, whenever our reflections slid across his icy black shades. One was a threat, 'No one waves a gun at my kids,' although we kids had never seen him wave his gun at us or at anyone else (and eventually, bored, we began to wish that he *would* wave his gun). And her other comment was the put-down, 'He fancies himself.' The beauty of this was that he was very obviously unfanciable. As far as I was concerned, everyone in the village was unfanciable.

On the Plaza, there was one shop, with a counter, which made life difficult for anyone who could not speak the language: 'Renee!' my mother would summon me from the doorstep, and give me her orders, 'two pounds of tomatoes . . .'

At home, I would not have had to do the shopping.

The first time, I objected, 'But they don't *have* pounds, here.'

'*Translate* for me, then!' she shrieked.

I had no notion of weights but I went sullenly, randomly, for a kilo, which seemed to do the trick.

There were no public telephones, so we had no contact with Dad unless we went after the evening's shopping to the telephonist's house and waited our turn to sit in the booth in her front room. When we came home from our first holiday, Mum complained to Dad, 'They can hear everything that I say to you.'

He said, 'But you're not speaking in their language, they hear nothing but noises.'

She tipped her sunburnt nose into the air and despaired. 'Shows how little you understand about communication.' Then she launched into, 'They starve their cats, and they're Catholics.' By this time she was desperate. 'They starve their cats but they call themselves religious,' she gabbled, 'and I'm

a heathen, you can see it in their eyes.' A heathen, bending
down in a short dress to stroke the Plaza cats, her wedding
ring skimming their spines.

Eventually Dad decided that something had to be done: he
decided that the next time he sent us to the *finca*, he would
send Auntie Fay with us. Auntie Fay was not our real Auntie,
she was a friend of my parents but particularly of Dad because
Mum did not have friends, not really. Women did not have
friends in those days, they had children. And Mum had a
lot of children. Auntie Fay was unusual because she had no
children. And she was useful because she went to Spanish
evening classes. Her husband was Dad's friend, or not exactly
a friend: he was an architect for whom Dad had done some
work. Auntie Fay worked for her husband, too, which was
how they had met and married: Dad told us that she was a
draughtsman, one of the best in the business. A lady draughtsman, he said. Mum said (and routinely told us not to repeat)
that Auntie Fay's husband was a boring old sod. If I had ever
met them, I did not remember.

I realize, now, that when Auntie Fay first came on holiday
with us, she must have been about thirty. I was thirteen, so
Mum was thirty-six. Layla was eleven, Alicia was six,
Yolanda, four, and Sebastian, two. Mum liked to explain the
five year gap between Layla and Alicia by saying, 'I had my
second wind when I was thirty.' Mum liked to refer to us as
a household of women (she did not count Seb, because he
was a baby rather than a boy, and babies are part of women).
Auntie Fay was one more woman: we were a *finca*-full of
women sent to the heat for the summer, grass widows in
reverse.

Auntie Fay was sent to keep us company but she came for the sun, below which she lay, naked, all day. Mum had always been a fanatical naked sunbather but would fidget, cursing the flies and her sweat, propping herself on pillows and tipping off loungers, or pacing the balconies, wobbling, in front of the french windows, to inspect and harangue her full-length and slightly distorted reflection. Auntie Fay lay still and small, she laid herself out on her towel and moved only in accordance with a precise schedule of exposure: she was aiming for an even tan, to the extent of including the underside of her arms. Sometimes when we came to talk to her, she would start to laugh as if she was being tickled, and shriek, plead, 'Get off me!' so that we soon learned not to cast our cool shadows on her skin. She was ash-blonde and pale-eyed but her skin did not burn. Which was lucky, because she did not believe in lotions, in protection, in dilution of the precious rays.

Her tanning, her non-burning, seemed like an act of will. After a week on her towel, she looked like the Bond girl who died of gold. During her second week, she worked on a darker finish. She darkened much more than I could manage in six weeks of sun. My skin was happy with gold, I reflected the sun with my light gilding of melanin, but her skin had to work much harder, to toughen and blacken to keep her safe and soft inside. Mum rarely came to the communal pool, but Auntie Fay never did so; she never came to see the rectangle of liquid marble, electric-blue and sun-veined, because the trip would have required clothes, straps, shadows, marks, and, anyway, water was sacrilege. Sometimes when she rose from her towel at the end of the day and wandered the patio to look at the view, we saw the fluorescent white flash of a Tampax tail. As the sun burned down into the hills, she liked to return to her towel to sit and see to her nails, twenty varnish-scented pearls which were quite unlike Mum's yellow horns.

In the evenings, she was a help with the shopping because she spoke some Spanish. What we wanted to hear from her, though, was her favourite expression, *Gott in Himmel*. We relished the accompanying impersonation of a Nazi: her thin nose became a bayonet thrust into the air, and somehow she seemed to make her eyes even paler than usual. Even Mum, who was a war baby and would not watch *Colditz*, loved Auntie Fay's quivering Nazi. Then, over time, the *Gott in Himmel* became more hilarious when it slipped into Auntie Fay's usual South London accent, a bored whine. But whenever we neared the Plaza, Mum would beg her not to say the words, not even in her London voice, not even *some* of the words (none of our faddy abbreviations, exclamations, *in Himmel*, then *Himmel*, and finally, simply, *Gott in*) because of the policeman.

'Faze –' Mum called her *Faze* '– remember, he has a gun, so don't, for God's sake . . .'

And we would echo, 'For Gott's sake . . .'

And Auntie Fay would promise: 'No laughs, then, today, for our laughing policeman.' Which made us giggle because this was so very unlikely: the policeman never revealed a glimmer of anything human, his expression was made for those twin black mirrors. So, whenever Auntie Fay filed with us across his dark shiny Plaza, she would settle for a mere, predictable, downward throwaway, 'Is that a gun in your pocket . . . ?' And our orderly procession would shatter into laughter; even the kids, to whom the joke must have been puzzling.

Auntie Fay's speciality, however, was Irish jokes. One evening, when Mum was weak with laughter but fortified with sangria, she wondered aloud if Auntie Fay was being unfair to the Irish. Auntie Fay replied, 'Listen, my *Dad's* Irish.'

We liked it when she told us about her family, about growing up: BC, she said, which stood for *Before Chris*, because Chris was her husband (the boring old sod, although we were not allowed to let on that we knew that he was a boring old sod). She told us about her old boyfriends, and we had favourites: we could never know enough about Emlyn, who, she had told us, was a location caterer, a *Croissant-server to the Stars*; and we were forever frantic to know more about why she had not married Clive, who had proposed to her in the pouring rain, shouting, 'Let it fall, let it fall,' as she had tried to dash for cover, then murmuring hotly into her hair, 'Drown, here, with me,' when she had come back through the puddles to him. Her story was that she did not marry him because his surname was Deed and she did not want to be known as Fay Deed, *Faded*. We did not know if she was serious. Her laugh was a growl because she smoked. She went outside to smoke, her exposed skin sprayed with insect repellent, whilst we stayed indoors and burned lozenges of mosquito-killer in the jumpy plugholes beside our beds. She stood on the other side of the french windows, on the balcony, her dark skin damp with repellent, and blew her own breathy smoke to the fat moon.

At the time I did not know how dangerous smoking was for Auntie Fay, who was diabetic: smoky sludge was lethal to her sugar-silty circulatory system. But cigarettes helped her to resist food, which was also lethal for her. Whenever she was on the balcony enjoying her mouthfuls of smoke, she could not hear us unwrapping and slurping *caramelos*. The first year that she came with us, she was newly-diagnosed and surviving without insulin. Or barely surviving, according to Mum, years later: reminiscing recently, she said, 'And do you remember, Faze was so weak that she could hardly sit up.' And I was surprised that not only did I not remember, but I had never known. To me, to us kids, Auntie Fay had seemed fine, or much more than fine, with her jokes and her relished nightly ritual of tan inspection, her purr of, 'Am I *brown*, girls? *How* brown?'

The doctors had told her to watch her food intake. Which meant that she sat in front of her precise portion and watched *our* food intake, our raiding of each other's plates. Mum would have determined our portions, braying about fairness and slimness. But when she turned away from the table, Auntie Fay would push some or most of her Mum-measured meal across to one of us, to the obvious loser. I did know that, day by day, she had to test her urine to track the level of sugar in her body. There was never any evidence of this procedure except the little box of sticks, for dipping, which looked not unlike her packets of cigarettes.

'Do you remember,' Mum continued to reminisce, recently, 'she was so weak that there were times when she couldn't get back up off the toilet, when we thought I'd have to go in there and drag her off.'

I do remember the mosquito bites: she was bitten much more than any of us, which, we decided, was because her blood was sweeter than ours. Her treatment of her bites became another nightly ritual, simultaneous with the tan inspection, but turning her prized dark skin candy-pink with calamine.

Her second summer, she had insulin: lots of little clear glass bottles lining a black box at the back of the bottom shelf of our fridge. So now there was a new ritual: injection. We watched the creamy sheen of her fingernails on her sun-polished thighs, stomach, or upper arm as she searched for a new site for the needle. She explained, and explained again and again because we wanted to hear one more time, that too many injections into the same patch would eat away her skin and leave a hole. We held our breath, knowing that her surface area was finite – more finite than most – so that sooner or later she would have to deal with holes. Then, to our relief, a new patch would swell between her thumb and forefinger and suddenly shorten the lowered needle. We never saw any hole; on the contrary, the skin would rise briefly as the needle came clean away.

Sometime during the summer, Auntie Fay taught me to inject her. I do not remember why, I cannot remember if I asked her. She taught me to concentrate on the syringe: before the insertion of the needle, I had to flick any obstructive air bubbles from the clear liquid; then before forcing the insulin from the syringe, I had to pull slightly on the plunger, to check the absence of blood in the needle, to ensure that I had not slipped into a blood vessel. These were the definite cautionary measures in the procedure. The actual sliding of the needle into her skin remained a mystery, but always seemed a success. For the moment that the needle was in place, I had to hold steady. I had to avoid the stir and tug of sharp steel in her skin. Sometimes she laughed, but motionless and low over the needle, more of a purr than a laugh, and muttered, 'Don't walk away, Renee,' slow and sharp like a private joke, but I hardly dared to allow myself a twitch of a smile. Then, 'Wow,' she would exclaim, but no louder, as the plunger squeezed the last drop of the dose into her skin, 'you'll make a wonderful nurse.' Which, in those days, I took as a compliment, and was, in those days, the best compliment that I had ever been given. When the tip of the needle had reappeared, thin silver from lush gold skin, I could see Mum's frown: she was fascinated, but unconvinced that this was a healthy holiday activity. Auntie Fay would say, 'I've never known hands like these,' and, 'they're steadier than my own.'

This was the summer when Mum discovered the local lepers. Somehow she found out that the white palace high in the hills on the other side of the valley was a sanatorium built at the turn of the century. It was run by nuns for people with leprosy who were sent by missionaries in South America. We were told that there were no longer any lepers in residence, or they were no longer infectious, or not from a distance, or not nowadays, or there was a cure: the accounts that Mum began to bring back to the *finca* were incomplete, muddled, contradictory, poorly translated from the local grapevine. And, in any case, she believed none of them. According to her, there were lepers in the hills and their disease was let loose in the air. And there was a direct airflow from the sanatorium to our *finca*; far superior, presumably, to all other lines of airflow in the valley, because no one else seemed worried. Or perhaps it was *she* who was far superior, perhaps the inhabitants of the local towns were so stupid that they had not noticed the loss of their fingers and toes over the decades. She paid no attention to other people, and became desperate to leave. But our return tickets were for two or three weeks' time. So we were stuck. With her. Most evenings, she telephoned Dad, and we had to wait for her, to sit by the amplifying booth with various villagers and listen – or try not to listen – to her repetition of the one word, *lepers*. Even Auntie Fay did not know what to say. Sometimes, when we looked across the tiny hot room to her, she would respond with a flicker of her Nazi impersonation, that deliciously ridiculous narrowing of her face and eyes; a last resort to try to make us laugh.

The days swam deep into August, airless under the heavy sun. Mum shut the windows and doors on the view of the white palace and the blue hills. She barred them not simply with the faint spangles of their wooden-framed mosquito nets, nor with their shadowy shutters, but with the glass panes which were usually left untouched until winter. In the day-time, she came outside with us because the air did not move even when we moved, but stuck to our skin and paved the patio. And she was prepared to risk a lot for a tan; there was no point to the holiday if she went home without a tan. But the winds came when the sun was gone, and then she preferred to stay indoors. Indoors, the air became hard to breathe. Sleep was impossible before we had risen from our beds, tiptoed across our tiled bedroom floors and opened our own windows. Mum did not seem to sleep. One morning I rose to find her on the balcony looking down over the town: during the night, one of the rare Saharan winds had come, carrying sand, to sprinkle the streets and stationary cars. 'See?' she proclaimed, her tone a weird mixture of exaltation and fear, 'I was right.'

But I wondered, 'About *what*?'

This had crept up on us: in the beginning, we had tried to ignore her, to carry on with our lives as normal. Auntie Fay had winked at me through the steam from one of her many cups of tea and whispered, 'Let it pass.' But it was impossible to remain untouched by Mum's frantic words and her relentless fastening of our windows; and she was forever fiddling with the kids' scabs, looking for signs. So Auntie Fay and I decided to find out more. But from where? Back home in England, Dad seemed to have discovered that leprosy was a bacterial infection. Auntie Fay and I knew that this meant that it was almost certainly true that there was a cure, an antibiotic. But this was irrelevant to Mum: she reported Dad's finding to us without any relief; worried, perhaps, not by death but disfigurement. Then, in the village, over coffee and crisps in a bar, a chatty expat told us, 'Leprosy is only very slightly infectious'; and another joined in, cheerfully, with, 'You're much more likely to pick up TB, here.' Which worried me because I had not had a BCG, I had not been allowed to join the queue of my classmates with their lopsided shirtsleeves because I did not have Mum's permission. Because she had been worried about scarring.

When we left the bar, Mum told us, 'You shouldn't believe everything that you're told,' by which she meant that we should not believe *any*thing that we were told. 'Who are all these sources of information, anyway?' she wailed, rhetorically, 'they're only *men*.' And none of us could argue with this. On another trip, to another town, we worked our way along a shelf of dictionaries in a bookshop until Auntie Fay could translate for us: 'The main symptom is a whitening of the skin.' She laughed, '*Well*, girls, I *definitely* don't have it.' But Mum decided, during the next few days, that Yolanda *did* have leprosy. So, despite our protests, she took us all to the local doctor on one of his days in the village. In his dark little room, she sat down and heaved Yolanda into her lap. We stood behind her chair, near the door. She showed Yolanda's nose to the doctor, pointing to the skin and saying, 'Not here before, *nada*, do you understand? *Comprende?*'

Yolanda's eyes narrowed on the fingertip until they crossed.

'Faze,' Mum panted, 'translate for me.'

But Auntie Fay could only say, again, sadly, 'Mags, I don't think there's anything wrong with her.'

Mum continued, to Auntie Fay, to the doctor, 'But she has never been like this before.'

The doctor leaned slowly and heavily over his desk, to pull and rub the skin on Yolanda's nose. Then, retreating, he shrugged wildly above Mum, and said a small, sharp word.

Mum called, 'Faze . . . ?'

'I don't know,' Auntie Fay admitted.

'*Que?*' Mum demanded of the doctor, '*Que?*'

So he repeated the word, twice. *Pecker. Pecker.*

Spanish for nose?

But beside me, Auntie Fay said, 'I don't know, I don't know.'

The doctor turned in his chair and pulled a heavy old book from a shelf on the wall behind him. He hummed a single note into our silence as he scraped through the pages, and then he pointed to a word, showed Mum, displayed the book to show all of us with his mottled fingernail: *Lentigo.*

'Lentigo,' confirmed Mum, and suddenly she began to chant, with determined calmness, 'Oh God, Oh God, *Lentigo, Lentigo.*' Just as suddenly, she asked him, 'What do we do?' but turned immediately to Auntie Fay.

Immediately, Auntie Fay repeated the question in Spanish. Another helpless shrug from the doctor: nothing.

'Nothing,' said Auntie Fay, superfluously.

But Mum was already saying, 'They don't care, do they? It's all *mañana* and *nada*, to them, over here. Life is cheap, here.' She stood up, dropping Yolanda to her feet, but the doctor half-stood with them and reached over his desk to press his huge palm briefly on Mum's forehead.

'Sol' he said, with a long, slow smile, 'mucho sol,' and removing his hand, he shook his head, *no*, *no*; indicating Yolanda, then indicating Mum with a laugh which cracked into a cough.

In his open doorway, Mum turned and said loudly to all of us, 'He smokes, did you hear his chest? What kind of doctor smokes? Well, let me tell you: a Spanish doctor.'

No one moved. Auntie Fay's top teeth came down on her lower lip; her eyes widened and did not blink. Then Mum took Yolanda's hand and they span from us down the corridor towards the sun-bleached open air. I picked up Sebastian, and Auntie Fay led the girls. When we reached the main doorway, we saw that Mum had stopped in the middle of the courtyard, that she was ignoring Yolanda and glancing around the buildings. She waited to hear the flap of our flip-flops in the dust before she commenced the lecture.

'This is a hard country; this is a country, remember, which fought a civil war, which is the very worst thing that a country can do.' She turned to us and urged, 'You must remember that, girls.' Marching ahead of us, she mused, darkly, 'Brother against brother.'

I squinted through the thick sunshine for Auntie Fay's wide eyes.

'I don't know,' Auntie Fay muttered in reply, but slowly, as if she was thinking hard.

Layla called after Mum, 'England had a civil war.' She was fairly new to secondary school, and to History, and still had enthusiasm for both.

From the corner of my mouth, I managed a quick, 'Shut up, Layla.' Which she caught full in the face, whirling her sun-speckled eyes to mine.

She bridled, 'Shut up yourself.'

Ahead of us, Mum stopped so suddenly that Yolanda bumped into her legs and bounced.

I hissed to Layla, 'Civil war is the least of our problems.'

Mum turned to us to emphasize, 'I meant, in my lifetime.'

And suddenly I had had enough.

'Not quite,' I corrected her, loudly; I was, by this time, an old hand at History. I had had enough of Mum's stories, I wanted some truth, and I wanted it loud.

Auntie Fay dropped Alicia's hand so that she could lay the iced tips of her fingers on my bare burnt shoulder, to remind me, 'It doesn't matter.'

But I had to tell her, 'It matters.'

And she gave up, shrugged, her fingers falling from me; she nodded, her eyes fixed on the shine of her pearly toenails in the dust which had lapped into her flip-flops. After a fortifying sigh, she looked up at Mum to ask, 'What do you want to do now, Mags?' and followed with a series of encouraging clucks for Yolanda, the terminal case, who took this as belated permission to cry.

Over Yolanda's wail Mum said, determinedly, 'We need to find help.'

Help was Alistair Emery, whose company Mum would not normally seek because there were rumours about boys. The rumours came from the other local expats, who specialized in rumours; but, for once, Mum did not want rumours, she wanted someone who knew something. And Alistair Emery knew a lot. Before his retirement, he had been a master in a famous public school. As we walked up the hill to his villa, I pondered the pricey education of public schools, the benefits of which we would now have, for free, for a few minutes. Would I pass Maths, if Dad paid? Could Alistair Emery explain molecules to me, and should I ask him?

According to Mum, he did not only know school subjects: she said that he had been in Spain for longer than anyone else, by which she meant any of the other expats, and so he knew every English-speaking source of expertise in the region; and much more importantly, he knew how to go home in a hurry. She said, 'He has his uses.' And then, occasionally, she continued, '*Lentigo*,' and, '*God*.'

After each *God*, Alicia piped, 'Yes?' Which was, to her, at her age, a joke.

No one else said a word, not even *Gott*.

Alistair Emery came onto his balcony to receive us with enthusiasm. I could not remember if I had ever seen him before: Mum talked so much about people that sometimes I confused her memories and mine. And this man was middle-aged, and in those days, all middle-aged men looked the same, to me.

'Mrs Paulin, Mrs Paulin, Mrs Paulin,' he announced, but this formal version was friendly, his equivalent to everyone else's *Mags*. 'And your friend, Mrs . . .'

Auntie Fay smiled and said, 'Lorne.'

'Mrs Lorne, Mrs Paulin, and your many lovely children.'

We had reached the top of the staircase. Cheerfully, Mum said, 'All girls.'

We all looked at her. And Alistair Emery looked at Sebastian, who stuck out his tongue, probably because this was what we had taught him to do when we stared into his face.

Mum's eyes were narrowed on Alistair Emery, but they widened wildly when she saw that she had failed to misguide him. She laughed, falsely, and said, 'Except Sebastian, of course; and what a terrible, terrible tomboy he is.' She laughed again, an even worse, even more false laugh; and the rest of us laughed, not much more normally, because Seb was so obviously not a tomboy. Seb laughed because he thought that the tongue had been a successful joke. So he stuck out his tongue again, but Mum shouted, *'Put that away.'* And then suddenly, belatedly, there was silence.

'Tea?' Alistair Emery asked, after a moment. 'Lemonade?' he asked Layla, Alicia, Yolanda.

His eyes skimmed Sebastian.

'No,' said Mum. 'Thank you.' She sank down on to a small wicker sofa, which mimicked the protest of her bones. She stayed forwards on the cushions, her elbows on her knees and her face propped in her hands. A suddenly small, suddenly white face. 'What we need is your help. We have been to the doctor and one of my daughters has *lentigo*.'

He frowned, gently. 'Are you sure that you won't have a drink?'

'We're fine.'

We were not fine. Yolanda began to cry, for all of us. Auntie Fay took her to a wicker armchair; they sat together, the armchair shuddering. I sat next to Mum, on the very tip of the flowery cushion. Layla tried to perch on the arm, but I swatted her away. She knelt on the tiles, copied by Alicia and then by Seb.

Alistair Emery said a conspiratorial, 'Wait there,' and went into the darkness of his doorway. In an instant, he reappeared, cradling a large new book. When he began to turn the pages, the smell of printers' ink was fanned across the balcony: a strange scent in a country where every smell is washed with bleach. As he turned, he was saying, '*Lentigo . . . Lentigo . . .*' which Mum began to say with him, wearily, an echo, but urging him onwards through the pages to the truth. Then suddenly he exclaimed, 'Ah!' and flourished a magician's smile. Raising the book, tipping back his head, he quoted, '*Another word for freckles*'.

Beside me, Mum moved slightly, I heard that she moved although I did not see exactly how, up or down. Expressionlessly, she said, 'Are you sure?'

He smiled widely, the smile of a sitcom vicar. 'Absolutely.'

Her expression was contracting into a cross frown. 'Let me see.' Her arm came across me, into the air in front of me, and stayed there.

'There's nothing *to* see,' he rejoiced, but gladly handed over the book.

Alicia piped, 'Mum thought that Yolanda had leprosy.'

Mum nearly went for her, her wicker screamed. 'No I did *not*.' Then, almost immediately, she closed the book and poked it at Alistair Emery, turned a smile on him, told him, 'But you can never be too sure.'

He said, lightly, happily, confidently, 'Oh I think you *can*.'

Politely, Auntie Fay enquired, 'Do you have leprosy in there?' She nodded towards his hands, the book.

He turned a frown down into the pages. '*Leprosy . . . leprosy . . .*' And during his new chant, he managed, 'May I ask: why the worry about leprosy?' He passed the open book on two wide palms to Mum.

She said, 'Because of the lepers,' took the book from him, did not look up.

But he did not stop his smile. 'Which lepers?'

'Up there.' She jerked her head towards the hills behind him, but no one saw her eyes.

'Oh no,' his concern bent him towards her, cut his tone to a whisper, 'none of them *have leprosy*.' Suddenly he flew close to a laugh, 'Do you think I'd live here if there was any danger?'

Her head, chin, came up; her eyes were narrow.

Hurriedly, he tried to explain, 'The institution is for rehabilitation. There are a few people who *have had* leprosy and are learning to function, so that they can come down here to live normal lives.'

Normal lives, down here? I looked at Auntie Fay.

Her silent reply was the opposite of her Nazi: a crumpled, barely contained smile.

As we walked away from Alistair Emery's villa – or *casa*, as he had seemed to prefer – Mum shivered and said, 'Don't you just want to go home and wash and wash?'

We knew that she was referring to Alistair Emery, not to the leprosy behind us in the hills.

Auntie Fay said, 'He's not after *you*, Mags.' Her voice was unusually faint, like a wheeze.

Mum stressed, 'Nor my son, if I have my way.'

Layla mused, 'No one's after Sebastian, he's too young.'

We went home to our *finca*, and, quite quickly, disease was forgotten: within a few days, Mum had returned to a state not wildly dissimilar to normal.

But there always seemed to be a death when we were away in Spain: one year, the pope – one of the popes, I do not remember which one; another year, Elvis. Mum's line on this was a swirl of wonder and dread: *Someone always dies when we're here.* And I would have to explain that this was likely because we were away for so much of the year: *someone* had to die, during those summers. We learned of these deaths by relying upon Auntie Fay's wobbly translations of the newspapers that were on sale in the town which we visited occasionally.

'Just think,' Mum breathed, again and again on the way home, when we had read the news of Elvis, 'if we hadn't come into town this week, we'd never have known.' These deaths brought us up sharp in the seemingly endless sequence of identical days. Elvis did not mean much to me: a dimply smile in clips and stills from cheerful old films that I had never seen; or the ballooning white catsuits, spotlit in the purgatory of Las Vegas. Neither Mum nor Auntie Fay had been keen on him, but the news made them remember other singers and actors whom they did mourn. Mum had tears in her eyes over Montgomery Clift. I was an equal in the reminiscence of one of *Alias Smith and Jones*; the cute, dark one. I joined in the lamentations over the shotgun which he had turned on himself. For a whole evening, our refrain buzzed with the drugged mosquitoes, and sank into our cups of watery, rind-sour sangria: *he was lovely; oh, he was lovely, wasn't he.*

The morning after the sangria, we woke to no water. Our

electricity supply was, by now, much more reliable, but we had problems with water. By the kitchen sink Mum sang out her bitter, disappointed, 'Here we go again.' The taps strained noisily. Instantly, I was thirsty, dirty, and much hotter than usual. I went onto the balcony to begin the routine: look for signs of tampering workmen on our land, and then for cars in the village below collecting from the common water supply, from the mountain spring. Up on our own hill we were usually the last to know about a problem, because somehow, contrary to all known natural laws, our pipes retained a supply for longer than anyone else's. We had to know if our problem was part of a bigger problem, or merely our own. I never knew which was worse: a bigger problem was ominous, but there was strength in numbers; but our own problem was a bigger problem, in a sense, because no one bothered about repairs for the British women on the hill, and we had no car to fetch supplies. As I was looking for clues, Auntie Fay came from the bathroom with two footless socks of white cream. 'I need water,' she said, calmly, perhaps fazed, 'because I'm de-fuzzing and I have five minutes before this stuff starts on my skin.'

'Look,' I pointed into the olive grove, to the man who was possibly the cause of the crisis and therefore our saviour. I could not see what he was doing, if he was doing anything, but he had a little van, he wore overalls of Mao-blue, and there were tools on the ground around him.

Standing next to me, Auntie Fay pushed me and said, 'Go, quickly, and ask him.'

He sensed our eyes, and looked around, across the crumbly terrace of tough thin trees, up to our balcony. He was young, he was a boy, his face and eyes smoother than any or indeed anything that I had ever seen in Spain. He was so very dark against the scabby glitter of the tree trunks.

I said, 'I can't.' Because I was wearing a bikini, and I was fifteen: I knew that I was a lump of pale puffy flesh stippled with stubble and mosquito bites.

She said, 'Just say *agua* and *quando?*'

'No –' *I know that* '– I have to go and put on my dressing gown.'

She protested, 'You look fine, you look lovely.'

And, anyway, 'I won't understand what he says back to me.'

So she turned and went down the steps, calling, anxiously, '*Señor . . . Señor.*'

As she stumbled towards him through the big dried clots of clay, he smiled harder and harder. But not at her foamy legs: he did not take his gaze from her wide, luminous eyes.

I was too far away to hear the conversation. On the balcony I could hear only the rattle of the thin dry leaves, like lizard's tongues.

Mum came on to the balcony, flat-footed with suspicion. 'What's going on?'

I turned to her but said nothing, suddenly I was sick of her questions. She could look for herself.

We turned together towards Auntie Fay, far away on the choppy soil, and she smiled and waved. Beyond her, behind her, the boy's head was nodding, bobbing, his black hair blindingly shiny. They seemed to exchange a few more words, and there was the splash of a laugh, netted by the squat trees. Then we watched Auntie Fay's brilliant legs as she waded back to us. For a moment, she disappeared beneath us, but unwound breathless from the spiral staircase on to the balcony to tell us, 'We'll have water now for five minutes, for me; and then he'll switch us back on, properly, in a few hours' time.'

Stepping aside for her, Mum wailed, 'What if he forgets?'

Auntie Fay strode past us, her legs burning but her eyes as calm and clean and unlikely in the sunshine as chlorine-sizzling pools. 'He won't forget.'

A few minutes later, when we were waterless once more, Auntie Fay came back to the balcony from the bathroom, and lay down near Mum and me. Lying on my towel, I could see the boy through the stony lace of the balcony wall and its openings for rainwater. Auntie Fay warned, 'Renee, you have shadows on you.'

'Good, because I'm hot.'

Mum said, 'Go indoors, then.'

But I did not move. The boy was busy, but I did not know what he was doing: the constant soundless clatter of his movements slid through the long moments like a breeze on water.

Mum murmured into the sky, to Auntie Fay, 'Your nice water-boy reminds me of Tommy Hale.'

But this boy was nothing like Tommy Hale. Tommy Hale was an apprentice joiner who sometimes worked with Dad: chippy, to Dad's sparky. He was always in our house, and not always when Dad was home. He was dark, yes, but in a pale way. His hands were pale, Mother's Pride pale. Rough with cuticles and splinters. There was no mystery to Tommy Hale. His eyes hopped behind Mum like hungry birds. And their whites were white, not washed turquoise like the eyes of the water-boy as they opened up, now, for me. The water-boy had moved to work below the balcony. I sat up, quickly, dropped the eyes. The sun was high, now, the sunlight running all over the sky. I burned with irritation: how could we sunbathe, with this boy so close?

Auntie Fay said, 'Get down, Renee, you're blocking my sun.'

I shifted across my towel and began to work suncream into my shoulders.

Auntie Fay mused, 'He reminds me of my lovely little brother.'

I hurried, 'Does he speak English?'

Her reply began with a laugh, which came as a cough because she was lying down and her lungs were lagged with smoke. 'Balham dialect.'

'Not your brother,' I explained, whispered. 'The boy. Because he's working beneath us.'

'Oh,' this was a sigh, followed by words which I missed, but which were happily dismissive, sounding something like, 'Let him be,' or 'Leave him there.'

I remembered that her brother's *wife* did not speak English. She was South American. For years we had been fascinated: *'How can they be married if they don't speak the same language?'* But Auntie Fay did not seem to think that this was a problem; she said that her little brother was the most happily married of any of her family. We loved her stories of her brothers and sisters, all seven of them. They were part of her growing up which was not merely BC: they were real, live, they were in daily contact from their different corners of London. Sometimes when they were children, when their father had gone and their mother temporarily failed to cope, they were taken briefly into care, as if they were going on a holiday. Anything but a holiday, though, and they went in twos and threes, diminished versions of the whole family. Yet

Auntie Fay managed to tell us a lot of funny stories from their times in care, stories of escape.

Usually, Auntie Fay was with us for a fortnight in the middle of our holiday, arriving and leaving by taxi. But this time she had come to us for our last three weeks, and was making her return journey with us. At the airport, she went with Mum to the toilets, and they were gone for a quarter of an hour. I had been left in charge of the luggage and the children. Layla had wandered off, Alicia and Yolanda had argued bitterly over and eaten all the *caramelos* which we were supposed to suck on the plane to help stop the pain in our ears, and Seb would not refrain from colouring the luggage labels with his crayons.

Eventually Mum came across the freshly swabbed tiles, and I complained, 'Where *were* you?'

Calmer than perhaps I had ever seen her, she explained to me, 'Faze has been crying in the toilets; she doesn't want to go home, to go back to being alone.'

There had been no secret: we knew that Auntie Fay and her husband were going to divorce, that he was going to marry someone else. I did not remember exactly when we had been told, between the jokes: we simply knew, it was a fact of life. For weeks we had heard Auntie Fay's mentions of this new life AD, After Divorce. And she had not seemed upset. Nor had the prospect seemed odd, to us: her husband had never been in evidence, and her life seemed full of her brothers and sisters and their various crises.

When Auntie Fay joined us, less than a minute later, her eyes looked smooth, not scoured by tears. Nothing was said, and we went slowly to the Departure Lounge, where she was waved ahead of us through Passport Control, ushered from our jumble of photos, names and faces, to bypass the strained Spanish head count. Framed in the plate glass view of the runway, she turned back, the frilled hem of her tiny dress fluttering against the lumbering, grounded planes; and, for me, as a Spanish soldier snatched my passport and scanned my face, she did the Nazi face, mouthed the word, *Himmel*.

AD, she fell in love with a Spaniard, the teacher of her evening class in Lewisham. So she stayed in Spanish Two for another year, even though her language was perfect.

She came to spend a week with us in Spain; only a week because she had a new job and did not want to take as much holiday as in previous years. In this new life of hers, time off was in short supply. She spent the week talking from her towel about the teacher, Fabian, his name pronounced in her perfected accent. According to her, the only problem with Fabian was that he would not marry her. Or not yet. So she would have to try harder, to work much harder on him. She tanned harder, during that one week, than in previous years; she tanned frantically to the hue of a blood blister.

I stopped going on holiday with the family, I was seventeen and did not want to spend my summers with my mother and the kids; and, anyway, Auntie Fay stopped, too, because she had her new life, a different life. She continued to see Fabian for years, Mum told me, but he never married her and eventually he went back to Spain without her.

I did not see her again for more than a decade, until she came to Yolanda's wedding. Yolanda, youngest of us girls, is the first of us to have married. She belongs to a different generation: my and Layla's generation, of baby boom babies, is the one that does not marry, or not when young, not until there is nothing more to do and we already have careers, homes, families. Alicia cannot marry her man because he is married.

At Yolanda's reception, I spotted Auntie Fay across the room. As far as I could see, the only change was that her blonde hair had been bleached blonder. She was standing with five or six people, she seemed to be telling them a joke or a story because their faces were broken up into laughs.

Her own laugh was rattling around inside her, she sounded rather sore. I waved to catch her attention. Her gaze switched onto me, and the eyes narrowed. And I laughed, thinking that she was beginning the Nazi face for me. Then I saw my mistake: she was older, her eyes were older, pale, her gaze was slack and she was simply trying hard to focus.

6

GUTS FOR GARTERS

I have met my cousin only once, twenty years ago. I was eleven and he was five. Not that anyone had ever referred to him as my cousin. He was *Connie's kid*. But I knew that Connie was my mother's sister, which made her kid my cousin. My mother never used *auntie* for Connie: even when I was small, I understood that she was deemed unworthy of the term. And there was even less mention of an uncle: whenever my sister or I decided to use *auntie* for Connie or *cousin* for the kid, my mother permitted this to pass; but on the few occasions – before we knew any better – when either of us tried to refer to an *uncle*, she hooted, '*Uncle! What* uncle?' This was before we knew the story, and we were puzzled: we knew about babies, so we knew that Connie's kid had had to come from somewhere – from someone – in addition to Connie.

Throughout my childhood I referred occasionally to Connie's kid as my cousin, but this did not seem to help, he seemed no more like a cousin to me. He was nothing like my friends' cousins, most of whom lived nearby and were no different from us. Those who lived elsewhere came to stay for summers and Christmases, bringing brand-new bikes and words, teaching us how to smoke and kiss. My cousin did not even live with my auntie and uncle; I had no auntie-and-uncle. I never knew how to answer that seemingly easy-to-answer question, *Do you have any cousins?* For many years

I chose to say no, and sometimes to go further and claim that both my parents had been only children. Which was true, in a sense, because what kind of sister to my mother was Connie? Eight years younger and disappeared when she was eighteen. The baby turned up a year later, but from then onwards no one knew whether Connie was alive or dead. If I told people the truth, that I had a cousin who was fostered, they seemed to think that there was a child who was fostered by an aunt and uncle of mine; not that there was a fatherless child of my aunt's who was fostered.

But he was fostered, from when he was a week old. And five years later, we went to see him. We were on holiday, in the countryside, in a caravan, and Dad decided that we should stay for a second week when he drove back home to return to work. I overheard the discussion from my fold-down bed: Dad told Mum that, 'There's no need for you and the girls to hurry home.' He told her that, 'This little break has done you the world of good.' All that she replied was a horrified, 'On my *own*?' But in the morning, when she told us that we were staying, she made this sound like her own idea.

A fortnight is a long time in a field, even in wonderful weather. As the days slowed and the grass shrank around the shiny wheels of the caravans, our meals were reduced to the packet soups which were all that remained of a supply that had included mixes for trifles and lemon drizzle cake. Eventually Blossom proposed that Mum should skip the seemingly laborious rehydration of these soups, their simmering and her watchful stirring. She suggested that we could enjoy the sparkly powders like sherbet dips, with drinks of water as cold as we could manage. Mum took this as a criticism, and yelled that she was not going to stand around in the village waiting for nonexistent buses and then drag hundreds of bags of sugary rubbish back from town for us. So she continued to frown over the temperamental Calor Gas cooker and we continued to live on her gritty soups and as many Mr Whippys as she would allow from the van which tinkled daily onto the gravel drive and parked humming in the shade of the sole tree.

Every evening, Mum would stumble away over the unfamiliar terrain of the field to phone Dad. Ten minutes later, she would return in a much better mood, singing odd lines from her favourite records, having been whisked back to her own world in that tardis of a phone box. But then, early one morning, from one of the ripped canvas chairs, I craned to watch her retrace her steps in daylight with more confidence. From the phone box, she made two calls: during the first call she was folded over the mouthpiece, her head on one side, her Biro tapping the coin box before she wrote very briefly; during the second, she was standing to attention even as she worried an insect bite on the top of one foot with the toes of the other, and she nodded emphatically and wrote for longer. When she returned, she enthused, 'We're going on a trip today!'

Blossom, who had drifted from her bed onto the warm metal steps in a cloud of sleep, was thrilled: 'To the pictures!'

Mum turned on her, 'We're not here in all this lovely fresh air so that we can spend all our time in some fleapit!'

'*Flea*pit?'

She announced, 'We're going on a train to see Connie's kid.'

Two trains, in fact: our windows scanned lots of villages and small towns, and I had an hour or so to invent futures for myself in every white house that dripped a froth of purple flowers. I did try to think about Connie's kid, but I knew nothing more than his name, Nathaniel, and the names of his foster mother and father, Miriam and George. Throughout the journey, Blossom was busy as usual with questions.

'Your sister...' quickly, shrewdly, she revised this, '*Connie*: was *she* pretty?'

Because the story was that Mum had been the prettiest girl in her class. Whenever Dad overheard her telling us this story, he would laugh and say something like, 'As if that's an *achievement*.' But, turning eleven, I was beginning to realize how much skill was necessary for conventional prettiness: the plucking, crimping, shading.

Mum considered. '*Fairly*. Not *bad*-looking. Although *I* thought that she had a squint.'

Blossom wriggled forward on her vast seat. 'Fairly?' She looked at me. 'Like Hermione?'

Mum turned to me, then back to reprimand Blossom: 'What a thing to say!'

I told Blossom, '*You* have *freckles*.'

Mum returned to me. 'Stop that; she's eight and I don't want her to grow up with a complex.'

Then she lectured Blossom, 'Once Hermione is blonde, her whole face will perk up; you wait and see. True, even, for me: since I turned blonde, I've never looked back.'

So, sometime in the future, like Mum, I would have to slap bitter-smelling sludge onto my hair, to wrap my head in an old towel for hours but still manage to scatter burning droplets over the bathroom carpet.

Then she added, wistfully, 'But Connie was clever, she had a prize for Latin, and she threw it all away.'

Blossom's face opened in horror. 'She threw away her prize?'

Mum snapped shut her eyes and drove her fingers into her black roots.

Blossom pressed on: 'What happened to her?'

Her eyes remaining closed, Mum said, 'You *know* what happened to her,' because, over the years, we had been told; but she obliged anyway, 'she ran away with a pop group.'

'But not like the Bay City Rollers?'

Eyes open, but vague, 'No,' wearily, 'you *know* not like the Bay City Rollers.'

'Like who, then?' Blossom unscrewed a Curly Wurly from where the tip was stuck between her teeth.

'I've told you: men with dirty long hair.' She folded her arms and muttered to the scenery, 'It was those bloody Beatles.'

I dropped a Toffo. 'She went off with *The Beatles*?' I had never heard *that* version before.

Mum whirled towards me with a click of her tongue, 'It was the *fault* of The Beatles. They put ideas into her head. They were pipsqueaks when they were Liverpudlians, but they were even worse when they began to take drugs and flounce around with Indians. I mean, Martha Reeves didn't feel a need to push her bed around the street, pronouncing.'

I did not know where to start with this, but Blossom chirped, 'Who's Martha Reeves?'

Mum merely despaired, 'Questions, questions, questions; one more, and I'll have your guts for garters.'

I remembered how, when she had told us that Connie had run away from her baby, Mum had complained, 'That stupid sister of mine couldn't look after a *hamster*.' And I had been confused, unsure if there had been a real hamster, if the hamster had been real. I was worried for the hamster, on and off, for some months. Mum had told us, 'Connie went off on the hippy trail,' and explained, or failed to explain, 'Morocco.' I knew nothing of Morocco, which I mistook for Monaco, for the location of the motor races that Dad liked to watch on television. And hippy *trail*? On the trail of some hippies? I had imagined hippies trailing their hair and beards and beads around the racetrack in Monaco.

Now Mum muttered to the branch-blurred window of the train, 'I hope Miriam's not Jewish.'

The toffee in Blossom's mouth rattled, 'What's Jewish?'

'Foreign,' she replied faintly to the window.

But I was not quite sure this was true. 'Elaine Bourne's piano teacher is Jewish and he's not foreign, he's a *cockney*.'

Mum turned to me, her eyes unusually wide and clear, '*I* was born within-the-sound-of-Bow-bells, and you know what makes me sick? That people think that we are so cheerful all the time.' She turned back to the window and complained, 'People think that cockneys spend their days going on about apples-and-pears.'

Blossom groaned theatrically, 'I *hate* pears, especially ones with *brown* in them. *Never* give me another pear.'

'I *mean*,' Mum continued, 'when have I *ever* said apples-and-pears?'

I ventured, 'But you do say Barnet and Boat Race.'

She turned on me, 'I *do not*.'

'You do. This morning you said Barnet; that was what you called Blossom's hair: her *Barnet*.'

Her hands clenched on the carrier bag in her lap. 'Well, that must have been *in passing*. I wasn't being *clever*.'

*　　*　　*

We had to walk miles from the station, the three of us trying to make sense of the directions that Mum had written down in a margin in her magazine, and which I read across into the printed words to try to amuse us: **Right** *exciting colour scheme for your kitchen,* **Straight on** *a cool surface.* Finally, turning into Lee Close, we saw that they were watching for us from behind their garden gate: a square woman beneath a mess of dark curls, a little boy who seemed to have the same hair, and a golden dog who was as big as the kid. Seeing us, they began to wave, the dog waving with his tail.

A few steps nearer, Mum called, 'Miriam?' The woman smiled even wider, the mouth pushing her cheeks line by line further into those crispy curls.

'Winnie! Come on in.'

Up close, the two heads of hair were very different: Miriam's darkness was dying away to grey, but every one of the little boy's curls cupped a buttery slick of sunshine. He could have come from an old-fashioned book, with his button nose and – I looked lower to check – the tiny rubies of a graze on each chubby knee. Next to those knees were Miriam's thick shins, driven down into solid purple ankles.

Mum announced, 'Nathaniel.' She was looking down, I could not see her face.

Miriam laughed as if the name was a joke, then immediately explained: '*Nat* is easier.'

Blossom's knees twitched with joy, '*Gnat!*' I knew from her knees that she had said *gnat* rather than Nat. Then she was saying, 'Look at this lovely dog, Mum!' and reaching towards the sleek blonde head which was tipping back to track her hand.

Mum slapped down the hand. '*Careful!* What have I *told* you?'

Miriam laughed again, 'He's fine,' and she told Blossom, 'his name's Goldie.'

The dog was dancing in front of us on his four thin legs, his front paws dabbing the long grass. He managed an appreciative touch of his nose to Blossom's fingertips, but her hand was not quite what he wanted, or not all that he wanted, he seemed to want something from all of us at once.

'*Nat*,' Mum was trying again, unsurely. I remembered that she had told me that she did not know who had named him: Connie, the maternity ward, the social workers, or Miriam. 'As in King Cole,' she added, slightly more confidently.

Blossom's face puckered, she was puzzled. 'Old King Coal?'

Mum touched my elbow as she told Miriam, 'This is Hermione,' before turning stiffly, reluctantly to Blossom, 'and this is Deborah.'

Blossom had hold of both sides of the dog's head and was rubbing his ears, the floppy triangles of orange velvet. The dog's eyes were closed, sunk into black patches that were not quite fur and not quite skin. '*Blossom*,' she informed Miriam. 'No one in the whole world calls me Deborah.'

Mum scowled down over her jutted chin. 'But it *is* your name.'

'Yes,' crisp and helpful, 'but Blossom's my name, too.'

'Not your *proper* name.'

'My *middle* name.'

Mum switched tactics, began to explain: 'I'd wanted a Hermione ever since I was a little girl . . .' How many times had I heard this? And every time she made me sound like a *doll*. '. . . so I'd had my choice; and then, second time around, I decided that I wanted a Blossom (postnatally, I was not-quite-right) but Hubby said that she should have a proper name.'

'*Deborah.*' Blossom opened her mouth wide, crinkled her nose, displayed her tongue, the root of her tongue.

Mum looked away. 'But Blossom stuck.'

Miriam purred, 'Blossom's a lovely name.'

Mum's hands went to her hair, her pale nails fluttered in her dark undergrowth. 'Oh,' she was dismissive, with a weary breath, 'it's only for family.'

'Oh,' Miriam's breath was the opposite, scooped back, 'you'd rather that we didn't –'

Mum realized her tactlessness. 'Oh, no,' the hurried insertion of a smile, 'Blossom is fine with us, if it's fine with you.'

Suddenly Miriam was walking away, leading us into her garden. 'One of my girls is a Petunia,' she called, cheerfully, over a chunky shoulder.

Mum perked up. 'Goodness! You were adventurous.'

Miriam laughed for a third time, louder, perhaps she had to laugh louder because she was further away. 'I wish I was: I didn't choose her name, she came to me as a Petunia.'

As soon as Miriam had settled us on a picnic blanket and gone to fetch drinks for us, Blossom wanted to know, '*Is* Miriam a Jewish, then?'

Mum was frantic to hush her, '*Shhh.* How do *I* know?' Then she hissed to me, 'How many kids do you reckon she has here?'

'Well, how do *I* know?' There was no sign of anyone other than the little boy, who was riding his bike on the strip of paving stones which surrounded the house, his stabilizers sounding brittle on the cracks. His cardigan seemed to have been knitted from a pattern for a baby, simply made bigger. He had very few places for a smooth ride: the garden, front and back, was mostly grass, unmown. Back home, we had a square of concrete for the dustbins and had to walk through the house to reach the back garden which was mostly a path down the middle and the whirly clothes drier. Our back garden had a splintery, sticky brown fence; here, we were hidden behind a hedge, I could smell the sunshine on the leaves, I could smell the warm wax on the shiny leaves.

Blossom said, 'He even has eyelashes.'

We turned to her; she had both arms around Goldie's neck, deep in his blonde ruffle. But his eyes were turned from her close gaze and his head held so high above hers that his firm black mouth sagged. From down here, he looked like a disdainful old man. From above, he had looked like a toddler, beseeching, following our eyes with his own, his black buttons with bone-coloured rims.

Mum merely muttered, 'What have I told you,' which failed to rise to the pitch of a question.

I looked closer. Goldie's eyelashes were nothing like his long white whiskers, each of which came from a big black freckle. There were so many of his tiny eyelashes that they made a stubby golden fringe above each amber eye.

Mum said, 'The only Goldie that you'll have in my house is a goldfish, and that's if you're lucky.'

I turned back to the house and saw that a woman had appeared by the side door in a dark-pink quilted dressing gown. Her bottom was pushed back onto the pebble-dash wall, but her head was dropped down and she looked caved in, or in pain. Her brown hair, so long and thin that it trailed to a point, had slipped forward to hide her face from us, but we could see that she was smoking, the cigarette cupped in her hand, beaded with her fingertips.

'Good *God*,' whispered Mum, 'who's *that*? Or *what's* that?'

'Petulia?' guessed Blossom.

From the house there were two loud strikes of steel onto crockery, accompanied much closer by a squeal from Blossom, '*Mum!*'

We whirled to her: Goldie's ears were tented, his head was on one side, and then suddenly he was galloping from us towards the house, his back legs bouncing behind him: time for his lunch, apparently. Blossom continued, 'Did you see his face? Didn't he look like a dog in an advert!'

The smoking woman did not seem to see him as he skidded through the door.

A few moments later, Miriam was wobbling on the doorstep with a laden tray. The smoking woman slunk behind her and was replaced by a girl who dropped down from the doorstep with Miriam. How old was this new girl? Younger than me, slightly? Her bones were much thinner than her joints; she was made of shoulders, elbows, knees, ankles.

Miriam called ahead cheerfully to us, 'This is Suzette, who is staying here with her mum for the summer.'

The girl's hair was the same colour as the trailing hair of the disappeared woman – dark, no particular colour – but was built, inch by precise inch, into a French plait. Her eyes were cupped by dim blue shadows, the darker, deeper streaks of which were slightly speckled.

Blossom twisted up onto her knees. 'That lady who we saw by your door?'

'Yes,' Miriam's breaths pushed hard into the heavy air; Mum rose to help her, to take the tray.

Behind them the girl ducked onto our blanket, cross-legged: one fluid movement, she was collapsible and now she was crumpled on our blanket, her head bowed over the butterfly of knees, the rope of hair slack between her shoulder blades. She linked her hands in her lap, a much more definite movement, but they pulled on each other, faded ink stains flitting on the dry skin, stains which were the same colour as the softnesses that I had seen around her eyes.

Miriam was checking with Mum, 'Will you all be okay to stay here in the sun?'

One of the blue-dappled hands flew to the girl's mouth, the tip of a nail slotted between her teeth.

Mum considered, 'Blossom has a tendency to burn.'

Blossom bellowed, 'I *do not*.'

Mum whipped around to her. 'You *do*.'

Blossom tipped her flaming nose into the air. 'I *do not*.'

Mum turned back. 'Well, burn, then.'

Miriam tried, 'You have lovely fair colouring, Blossom.'

Blossom said, '*Mum's* dyed.'

Mum breathed a mixture of a laugh and a sigh, '*Kids*,' and one hand fluttered over her white-hot hair.

On the tray there were six tall glasses, a taller glass jug of cloudy liquid, a mound of sandwiches and a fan of paper napkins. The bread was brown, very, and had been sliced thickly by hand. Each filled chunk had been cut only once into two halves, these cuts swollen and tender with wavelets of cream cheese or sinewy tomato. Miriam introduced the sandwiches to us, guided us through the formation on the plate, 'Cream cheese, cream cheese and cucumber, cream cheese and banana –'

'*Banana?*' shrieked Blossom.

'You don't like banana?'

She looked affronted, 'I *love* banana.'

'Oh,' Miriam laughed, 'good. And these are tomato and pickle.'

'Branston,' Blossom muttered, slightly unsurely, looking at the sandwiches.

'No,' Miriam had to tell her, 'not Branston, I'm afraid, but Miriam.'

'Oh,' Blossom's puzzled look came briefly to Miriam, then returned to the sandwiches.

The little boy settled next to Miriam, held his cream cheese and banana sandwich in both hands. Miriam told us that the drink was lemonade, but the cloudy liquid was different from the lemonade that we had at home: not fizzy, and with the taste of lemon, both sharp through the skin of my mouth and clinging.

'And for pudding,' Miriam told us, 'I've made some ice-cream.'

Made?

'With the strawberries that we picked yesterday,' she added, turning to the girl, who nodded.

So she *did* mean that she had *made* the ice-cream, not that she had merely come up with her own mix of flavours and toppings bought from a shop.

I had to know more: 'You *made* ice-cream?'

'Strawberry, my favourite,' she replied, cheerfully.

Blossom whooped, '*My* favourite,' which was not quite true, because she claimed every flavour as her favourite.

'But how can you *make* ice-cream?' Because ice-cream was something that spiralled down from silver machines in musical vans, or came rippled in boxes from freezers in shops. How could she make something that was frozen?

She could see no problem: 'Well, you make up the mixture and then freeze it in the freezer compartment.'

Blossom whirled around to Mum, 'Can *you* make some ice-cream?'

Miriam came to Mum's aid, '*But* it *is* a bother, you have to keep stirring the mixture, every hour or so for hours and hours, or you'll end up with a solid icy block.'

'*So*,' Mum told Blossom, with a clipped smile, 'your answer is *no*.'

The ice-cream came in a Tupperware box; we peered down into the box to see a filling which was too pink to be true, party-dress-pink, and winking maroon pips. Miriam levered portions from the smooth rectangle with a serving spoon, each gash slightly furred with ice. This ice-cream had more flavour than strawberries, Miriam had done something – how had she done this? – to distil the flavour. My tongue held each mouthful onto the roof of my mouth, to warm, to squeeze more strawberry from the stubborn ice, the slippery cream.

When I finished, I was reclining, propped on one elbow; I sank down onto my back and closed my eyes, watched the sun burn onto my eyelids. I heard Mum's hands move around inside her bag, then Miriam's decline of an unspoken offer of a cigarette, 'Not for me, thanks.'

Mum agreed, 'I'll give up soon, this is *not* something that I want to be doing when I'm old; I reckon thirty-five is too old to smoke,' and she added, in explanation, 'three years' time.'

Now the rasp and fizz of the match, its dark blue burn of

the air. How many cigarettes in three years? The deep smell of the match was smothered by a slick of tobacco smoke.

'Because I've had to watch what happened to Dad.' Mum's voice again, talking about Grandad.

I opened my eyes; the sun had disappeared behind the girl's head, but sunshine ran down the plait which had popped over one shoulder.

Miriam said, 'Yes, I was so very sorry to hear about your father.'

'Oh,' a dizzying inhalation, 'you know, he was *told* to smoke, by his doctor. In the olden days. To help him to breathe. He was ill for years.'

Looking at the girl, I saw that there was a smile in the shadows of the back-lit face, and that this smile was focused on me.

I asked her, 'Do you go to school around here?' *Was* there a school around here, out here in the country?

'No, because it's the holidays, but I suppose that I will if we stay.' Then her eyes were washed away behind her eyelids.

Behind me, from Mum, came the muted whistle of a blow and the sickly smell of a tunnel of smoke.

'The last four or five years have been very hard on my mum.' Grandma: I pictured Grandma, her piled-high white hair like a Mr Whippy on her head. Her home-made toffee which she broke into pieces for us with a special tiny hammer. I was struck that Grandma, Grandpa, could never have come all this way, from London to here, to see the little boy.

I asked the girl, 'Where's your real home, then?'

'We were in a caravan but there was a fire.'

'*We're* in a caravan, but for our *holiday*.' I rocked myself up onto both elbows, to look closer at her: 'Are you a gypsy, then?'

'No,' the eyes returned, the mouth became as round as the eyes, 'we had to live in the caravan because we did have a room, but the landlord told us to move.'

Down beside me, the dark reflection of a bird crossed the shiny surface of the tray.

Mum was telling Miriam, 'You know that Dad had his own shop?'

I told the girl, 'At home, we have a land*lady*.' But could our nice Mrs Gresham ask us to leave? Could she seem to be our friend – dropping in for cups of tea – but then ask us to leave? Because what if she decided to live in our house? What if Mum had made our house so nice that Mrs Gresham decided to return? I did not think that we could live in a caravan. I had to know, 'Did you have a telly, in your caravan?' Because this was my chief complaint about our caravan: no telly.

'No,' then her face rounded, 'but we have one here.'

Mum was saying, 'He had to sell up. That shop was his whole life. Had been our home.'

Now I wanted to know, 'Do you have any friends, around here?' I could hear no one in the neighbouring gardens. I wanted to know what would happen to me if I was moved to the middle of nowhere, I wanted to know how I would survive.

She tracked a colour in the tartan of the blanket, then looked up and the blue of her eyes rippled. 'There's Miriam and Nat,' then came the laugh, a popped bubble, 'and Goldie.' She was laughing but I could see that she was serious.

I asked her, 'Do you want to stay here?'

The blue became smooth. 'Yes.'

Mum continued. 'And Asians took over. And now the shop smells Asian. The old smell was – what? – I don't know – vanilla, soap flakes, dust, I don't know, *nice* dust. And now the place smells of Asians. And I think that Dad felt responsible.'

The girl hunched, lowered the knob of each elbow onto each knee, lowered her chin into raised, splayed hands. 'But the Council will find us a new home, when Mum is better.'

'Oh.' So, her mum was ill, which explained her appearance in a dressing gown in the middle of the day.

Mum was saying, 'We were brought up in that shop. And everyone knew our business. So, yes, we had to behave, and, yes, Dad had standards, but he was *fair*, he *was* fair.'

There was a silence, in which I asked the girl, 'Is your mum okay?'

Her two front teeth peeped, testing her lower lip. 'She has to stop worrying,' she confided.

Mum was telling Miriam, 'The problem was that they had Connie too late in life; that was the problem, I think.'

The girl continued, 'She worries about everything,' this came much more quietly, close to a whisper. 'People. Shadows. Voices. Ghosts.'

'*Ghosts?*' This was ridiculous. 'But ghosts don't *exist.*'

Mum was saying, 'My husband isn't happy to have her name said in our house.'

The girl told me, 'The worries are like bad dreams, but when she's awake.'

'She sleepwalks?' I remembered that Mum had a story about once having found Blossom on the stairs in darkness and asking her where she was going, to which Blossom had replied gravely, 'To the yacht.'

I asked Suzette, 'What do you do with her? Take her back to her bed?'

She thought for a moment, suddenly still, not quite frozen. 'I try to tell her that everything's okay, I suppose. And to carry on as normal.'

This is as far as I have remembered. And until now, until I tried harder, all that I had ever remembered was the snapping away of that Tupperware lid to reveal the ice-cream, too pink to be true, flush with the walls of the box. Frozen yet malleable, frozen on a hot day, boxed pink sheen on a day rich with shade. The strawberries' raw redness tempered by cream. The taste of those invisible, disappeared, drowned strawberries. And Suzette: the dark spine of hair; the knuckles which were pearls; the deep-water blue around her sunken eyes. And her mother in the distance, shuffling, smoking, worrying. I had remembered next to nothing of the little boy, or of Miriam.

Mum never did give up the cigarettes. Eventually they gave up on her, but only when there was no more air in her for them to burn away. And now, like a virus, the cigarettes have moved on. To Blossom, for one.

Today I rang Blossom to ask her if she knew anything about Connie's kid. To ask if, perhaps, she had an address for him. I had forgotten to ask Mum before she died; because there had been so much else to do. Over the years, from time to time, she had mentioned him, and so I knew that his foster father had died, followed a year or two later by Miriam. Mum had said, gravely, 'Of course, they never had been young.'

'Deborah,' I said, 'it's Hermione.'

I heard the blip of surprise in her reply, 'Oh, *hi*, Hermione.'

After some pleasantries, I asked her: 'I was thinking: do you know what happened to Connie's kid?'

'Haven't a clue.'

'There's no address for him, or anything?'

'Not that I know. The last that I knew, he was living near Bristol with a sister.'

'A *sister*?' Connie had another kid?

'Not a *real* sister: step, or whatever, I suppose.'

I asked her, 'Do you remember when we went to see him?'

I could almost hear the frown. 'I don't think that I've *ever* seen him.'

'We were on holiday, somewhere in a caravan and Dad left us there –'

'Well, *that* figures.'

'– for a week, and one day we went on the train to see Connie's kid. A *hot* day: we sat in the garden with him and Miriam and another girl, Suzette, who was staying there with her mum, and we had home-made lemonade and strawberry ice-cream.'

'No,' she considered. 'Sounds nice, but rings no bells, I'm afraid.'

A few minutes later, though, when we were saying our goodbyes, there was a sudden squeak, 'Did they have a *dog*?'

'Yes.'

'*Ah*,' she relaxed, 'I *do* remember the *dog*, he was *lovely*.' And she finished, 'I'd *love* a dog like that,' adding, cheerfully, probably to herself, 'one day, eh?'

7

SLIPPING THE CLUTCH

It was said, in my family, that Uncle Robbie *cut a dash*. But said grudgingly, with suspicion. Then it was added with relief that he was *not blood*. He was married to my Auntie Helen, my father's little sister. No one in the family had a good word to say for him, except for Auntie Helen, but the best that she could do was to say that he was *worldly*. I was seventeen when he turned up. *Like a bad penny*, my mother liked to say, which made no sense because he was new. We had never seen him before, then suddenly he was due to marry Auntie Helen. In the piggy bank of bad pennies that had been Auntie Helen's life, Uncle Robbie was the worst and he stuck. I was seventeen and impressionable, he was twenty-six; he was impossibly and deliciously old for someone who seemed to know everything about anything that was important to me when I was seventeen. Which was love, mainly, I suppose, and ambition. And cars. He drove fast cars, and drove them fast.

But most importantly, Uncle Robbie was beautiful. I had never seen a beautiful man, before; or not one who was not made from celluloid. His cheekbones were so prominent that they seemed to precede him into rooms. They almost frightened me. His eyes were the colour of shallow water, they had the shine of water and water's trick of moving without going anywhere. His smiles slipped lazily sideways, they could have been whispers that I did not quite catch. I was an only child, and, until Uncle Robbie, men had been mere teachers or dads: men who were strapped with bulky watches and tied into grim shoes with socks which seemed wrong, socks which were somehow both too short and too long. Even the sounds of these ordinary men were alien to me, their noisy nose-blowing and throat clearing.

Over the years, I met up with Uncle Robbie on family occasions, which were occasions that we both wished to avoid: especially Boxing Day lunch, which, unfortunately, my family tended to interpret literally. This was during the seventies, when style was in short supply, and on these occasions my mother would hector me: *Miranda, must you wear those eyelashes/boots?* Uncle Robbie's dress sense worried me: he reminded me of photos of my father during the fifties. He was more successful than me in his efforts to avoid the gatherings, mainly because he was older, so no one could tell him what to do. Sometimes no one even knew where he had gone. And then the word from Mum, coming away from the phone, was that Auntie Helen was *hysterical*. She did not say *drunk*, which was the truth. In those days, I was faintly amused by these scenes, relayed in earnest by Mum; but in retrospect I pity my Auntie Helen, who did not always know something as basic about her husband as his whereabouts.

Whenever Auntie Helen and Uncle Robbie turned up to a family occasion, Auntie Helen would, in my mother's words, *make an effort to make an effort*: the fixed smile; the sparkly clutch bag in one hand, the Babycham glass in the other. But Uncle Robbie seemed to stand apart. Usually with me. He took me away from them, took me out of myself. He made me laugh, which I did not often do when I was seventeen, eighteen, nineteen, or not properly; I did a lot of laughing, from time to time, but not very happily. And certainly never with grown-up men. What did he say to me? Nothing very much, I realize now. I suppose what was special was that he bothered to talk to me at all. Or, what was important was the smile which came with the words. Unfortunately, in reply, I tended to talk a lot, never having had anyone to listen. Once, I remember, his smile stopped me in the middle of a monologue so that he could check, 'Oh, yes? and what do you know about love?'

I shrugged – *What do you want to know?* – and replied, 'Conquers all? Is a many-splendoured thing? Means never having to say you're sorry? The course of, never runs smooth?'

And he laughed, 'Well, I see that no one can teach you anything.'

But Mum, lurking and overhearing, which was her primary function in life, disparaged, '*Words*. What Clever Clogs needs to learn is what they *mean*.'

What Uncle Robbie had done with his life, so far, was to defect from academia to the City. He had been a mathematician (not simply clever but, of course, in the words of my family, *too clever*). His justification for the defection, he explained to me, was that he had never been a *pure* mathematician. Which I repeated to Mum, who was too ready to agree: her version was that he had been *seduced* by the City. And apparently this seductive City accounted for his clothes: Mum complained that he was *a dandy, down to his wedding ring*. Her chief charge was that he sent his shirts somewhere to be laundered. She meant somewhere other than Auntie Helen. I sensed that his pink newspaper was scandalous, too. This newspaper was linked with his job, which my parents dismissed as *up-market gambling*; or, *no better than gambling*. Gambling seemed quite good enough, to me. Certainly it seemed to work for Uncle Robbie, who preferred the term *Risk Analysis*. Who loved risk. Whenever Mum returned to her theme of *bad penny*, Dad would add, *And let me tell you, no penny that he has ever had has been anything but bad.* But Uncle Robbie had so very many of those pennies. My parents were fond of conversations about *standards of living*, which were, in fact, conversations about washer-dryers.

Sometimes I tried to ask Uncle Robbie about his own family, but his replies were evasive. On one occasion he replied with a question: 'Remember the father in *Mary Poppins*, before he becomes nice?'

I nodded, vaguely.

'Well, *both* my parents are like him.'

Was this an answer? What did I remember about the father in *Mary Poppins*? His bowler hat, his job in the bank. So why try to follow in their footsteps? I was too young, then, to understand about footsteps, that the choice is to follow or not to follow, which, somehow, is no choice at all. Our family knew from Auntie Helen that his family did not like her: she said that, in their eyes, she was a *tinker*. I wondered, but did not like to ask: what, exactly, was a tinker?

When I was seventeen, I was made of dreams, the most pressing of which was to learn to drive. But not in my father's Opel Kadett. So, at one of the family gatherings, Uncle Robbie offered to teach me in his car, which was, at the time, an Alfa Romeo. The offer was secret, he asked me to tell no one in the family. Over several years, I had occasional lessons and drove a succession of absurdly expensive cars in all the usual places, in empty car-parks, on overgrown air fields, in City streets on weekends. The stereo played Gluck, which he said was the sound of angels, and, similarly, Roxy Music. Our lessons were so infrequent that I never improved, but I never went to anyone else, never considered going to anyone else; in fact, I remained loyal to my initial instructor until I was in my thirties, when I could delay no longer and had to find another.

Uncle Robbie's cars failed to teach me very much because I could hardly sense that I was driving: they had so much power that they seemed to drive themselves. To reassure me, he would remind me that everyone else had brakes. I was particularly uneasy whenever I had to give way: he tried to teach me not to stop – not even when the sign insisted that I should STOP – but to slow down and hold back until the moment when I could speed forward. On the whole, I did not do well except for the parking. I parked so well because I was always so pleased to have stopped. Uncle Robbie liked to proclaim that I could park on a sixpence. The sixpence amused me: sixpences had not been around for years. But, then, Uncle Robbie seemed to come from a different era. Or no particular era at all. The mystery is that the only words and warnings that I remember from those hours in his cars could have come from anyone: *Clutch control . . . Indication . . . Anticipation . . .*

Throughout those years, I had to wait for him to come to me. Once, when I had not had a lesson for a while, he came to find me at university. Which, I suppose, was not so very far from home, an hour up the motorway, or, in his case, in his car, half an hour. I was pedalling my bike to a lecture when I was cut up by a Ferrari. Uncle Robbie lunged to open the passenger door, and announced, 'Revision, today: three-point turns. Get in.'

I began to fuss, to look for somewhere to chain the bike.

'Leave it,' he told me. 'If it's gone when we come back, I'll buy you another one.'

And I did as he said, I do not know why. My battered bike was the most expensive purchase I had ever made. I did not know if he was serious. He was smiling, so perhaps he was joking. But he tended to smile when he was serious, too. And he loved to trust to luck. Which worked very well until the end. Nowadays I realize that I would never have been insured to drive those cars, hence the secrecy.

My parents liked to say that he was *supremely unreliable*. Which seemed wonderful, to me, in my world stocked with parents and teachers and boyfriends who were supremely reliable. But nevertheless, somewhere along the line, I made the fundamental mistake of relying upon him to be there, for me – somewhere, or anywhere, or perhaps simply *to be* – and when I was twenty-four, he defaulted on me and died. He drove a Lagonda into a tanker. For days, Auntie Helen said very little except, *I didn't know anything about a Lagonda*. As far as she had known, his latest car was a Porsche: the plain old top-model Porsche to which he had become entitled when he became a partner. But, then, what did she know, by then? Because he was no partner of hers: they had been separated for a couple of years. The separation had been amicable, with no mess, like the contents of an egg. She had said that she could not live with him any more, and he had moved out. And so I had learned that this was the way of the world: the woman stays, the man moves. He had moved into a flat in Notting Hill, an area which my family dubbed *shady*. I did not know the area, but I realized that they were not referring to foliage. I had his phone number but – because I was grown-up, and because, ultimately, despite them, he was a member of my family – I had had little contact with him in his last few years.

But I was home when he died. I presumed that I had come home for the day because I had nothing else to do, even though I had had several months of nothing to do and had never even dropped by. I did not know that I had come home for him to die. Mum took the call; she came away from the phone without a word, which was unusual. The manner in which she replaced the receiver and backed away from the phone was unusual, too: she was rigid, not supple with speculation and insinuation.

'What?' I demanded to know, from the living-room doorway.

Absently wiping imaginary mess from her hands onto an imaginary apron, she looked around but, without seeming to see me, she replied, 'I'm sorry, but Robbie has died.'

She had never called him simply *Robbie*: she had always said *Uncle Robbie*.

She said again, 'I'm sorry.'

Which made me self-conscious, pinned into the open doorway: I felt that I should reply, say, *Oh, that's okay*.

But I said nothing, and then she told me as much as she knew from the phone call, from Auntie Helen, which was not much: the Lagonda, the tanker, the ambulance, and that he was dead-on-arrival, which sounded like dead-on-time and confused me. I was saying *yes* to everything, I said *yes* whenever it sounded right, because I wanted something to sound right, and, surprisingly, I wanted this to be easy for Mum. Or perhaps, simply, easy for someone. And I was lulled by the hum of our voices, until, eventually, I started to worry: *Did she say that Uncle Robbie has died?* And I did not like to ask. Because if he *had* died, then she would think me very odd for checking so late in our conversation; and if he had *not* died, then she would think me even odder – she would think my question in very poor taste. So I listened more carefully, for a few seconds more, until I was certain that he – his death – was the topic of our conversation.

Then Mum excused herself, politely. This was the first time that she had ever been polite to me apart from after my appendectomy, when I had come around from the anaesthetic to hear her formal enquiry, *How are you?* As if my stitches had somehow placed me beyond her, or made me into someone new. Now, in the hallway, she explained politely that she had other people to tell, to phone: Dad, who was at work, and Grandma, and a lot of aunties and uncles, the whole family; *the whole caboodle*, she said, strangely, inappropriately, but she had always had problems with words when she was under stress. I went back into the living-room, and resumed watching television. Because I did not know what else to do. Eventually I became hungry, but did not know if I should eat. I did not want to think of food, or even to be hungry; I did not want to think or feel anything that was not focused upon Uncle Robbie. My gaze slid around *The Young Doctors* and I listened to Mum, to her repetition, to the syncopated rhythm of story and silence, the gaps in her delivery which were Dad, Grandma, the aunties and uncles. In a sense, she was telling them what they already knew, because they had always said that Uncle Robbie would *come to a bad end*. And surely there is no worse end than the back of a tanker. The tanker, I simply could not find my way beyond that tanker; I wanted Uncle Robbie, I trawled my mind for a sense of him, but I kept coming up against *the tanker*. What I did not understand was that I did not yet miss him. That to miss someone takes time.

Later that day, there was distant lightning. Mum called to me to turn off the television, her usual precaution: her fear was that the television would channel the chaos of the sky into our house. I obeyed, then went into the garden, to watch. I saw the sudden bone-china cracks on the black-lacquered horizon. Then I heard Mum's voice, flying from a doorway: 'What are you doing out there? It's dangerous! Come back!'

As I came towards her, she complained, savagely, 'Don't I have enough worries?'

She was cooking, and I sat down in the kitchen to watch her work on the pizza dough. She massaged the warm brown bundle, which was then thrown around and slapped like a newborn and stubbornly lifeless baby. At one point, she paused, almost smiled and exclaimed, almost apologetically, 'So much *kneading*.'

The pizza was for Auntie Helen, who arrived a few hours later. The mystery, to me, was what she been doing for those hours. Crying, by the look of her eyes. She was going to stay with us; because, Mum had explained to me, she could not simply *be left*. Mum did not seem to know how long Auntie Helen planned to stay. Nor did Auntie Helen. Or, she had no plans. And of course she had no plans. In fact, she did not even have an overnight bag. When Mum asked, 'Where

are your things?' she wailed, 'Don't bother me with details.'
Mum offered her own clothes, but Auntie Helen said that she
would prefer to borrow mine. Her professed reason was that
she was closer in age to me than to Mum. As if we were
children, as if our clothes were children's clothes, *24 yrs*,
31 yrs, *45 yrs*. Dad was home from work by the time that
she arrived, and I heard him whisper to Mum, 'She's half-cut.'
After that day, not only did I never see her drunk again, but
I never even saw her with a drink.

After her first few days of stunned near-silence, Auntie Helen
leaked details for weeks. She had tapped the paramedics, the
police, the firemen, and the coroner for their versions. So
I learned that Uncle Robbie had died, desperately, in the
ambulance; the siren bawling, and the thick, low sky scoured
by the rotating beacon of antiseptic toilet-cleaner blue. The
tanker had borne the word *Non-hazardous*. I knew that it
was odd for Uncle Robbie to have hit the tanker because if
there is something that a Lagonda can do apart from speed,
it is *stop*: the brakes, like everything else, are extremely
powerful. But, in the end, weather conditions are everything:
the stains on the road were blacker and hotter than blood,
they were skid marks. Uncle Robbie held on long enough for
the paramedics to reach him, but then they could not hold
him together. His liberated blood filled both airways, his own
and then their plastic version. He flickered, occasionally, with
so much needing that his hands and mouth and eyes reached
for lifelines but pulled too hard. So that the paramedics had
to fight him back down. In the end, he filled with his own
blood, drowned in his own blood. *Filled*: Auntie Helen
seemed to want to impress upon us how terrible his death

was, but we already knew. During the weeks that she stayed with us, I left a lot of meals half-eaten.

But often I simply had to sit and listen; *someone* had to sit and listen, and everyone else was busy with arrangements. Her principal complaint was that, *It was not supposed to end like this*. I was amazed that she should have had an end in mind, I was too young for endings, I was unable to think that far – I had no vision of the future that was not a remnant from childhood day-dreams. I did not know what to say to her, but I sympathized, my gaze gloved her cold hands on their sweeps through her unwashed hair – increasingly unwashed – and in their clasps of her arms and shoulders, their search for memories of him. *In my clothes*. I did love her, but it was hard for me to see her crying in my clothes, because I felt that, in the words of the song, *It should have been me*. All this time, I could not speak my story, my version: he had been my first love, my first ambition in love. I had been so much younger, so I had put up with the inevitable procession of clammy boys, which was far from exciting (although sometimes, in desperation, I had found ways to liven up the proceedings). And sometimes, *only sometimes*, my heart had been shot down by one of those silly boys. All this, I did for him. I had been waiting for him. I had never quite given up on him, I had been certain that our time would come. All those wasted years, and now no hope of redemption. I had decided that it was permissible to have such intentions for him because he was not blood. And he was not married to Auntie Helen, not really, not any more: she had had what she had wanted of him, and she had had enough. I had a habit of saying to my friends, *I love him to death*. This was slightly flamboyant, only slightly, but nevertheless his untimely death was my

comeuppance: my words had been prophetic, I had been pun-
ished, I had killed him with my deadly, incestuous intentions.

I was twenty-four and a mess. I had grown up and stopped,
and started going nowhere. I had lost my job, recently, and
left my boyfriend. Of course, I had not been expecting Uncle
Robbie to sort out my life for me; but had I got around
to ringing him, I would have expected sympathy, empathy,
solidarity, or something. Because we were kindred spirits.
Now I was going to have to do this on my own. He was
thirty-three and very much more of a mess. Throughout the
funeral, my eyes returned from the many young women in
little black dresses to the coffin, which seemed suspiciously
small for him. Uncle Robbie, *large as life*. I thought of plane
crashes, bodies largely unrecovered and coffins filled with
sand. And, in a sense, this was a comfort: the thought of him
not inside the neat pine box, not held down by his own dead
body.

Mourning is a dreary business. Chronic, like drizzle. Physi-
cal, like a stitch. And lonely. I held no hope of recovery, nor
any memory of happiness: no way forward, no way back, I
was nowhere. And I was weary with computations: *a week
since he died*, *ten days*, *five weeks*, *four months*, an obsession
with distance which was, I suppose, on the contrary, a way
to hold on to him. I saw bits of him sometimes in the streets,
in other people, and followed them: his eyes, almost, his smile,
but not quite. Never the whole of him. Simply to see him
would have been enough, if only for a moment. Was this too
much to ask? Eventually I worked out how to do so: if
I could travel far enough into space, to a star, and then
look back to earth, I would see nothing but our old starlight;

and so, from the correct distance, with the appropriate tele-scope, I could see into the past and find him. This stood to reason.

When I began to feel better, my improvement was unpredict-able – a good day followed by a bad day – and therefore demoralizing. I spent my evenings frowning at stars, pondering distances, and no one ever talked to me about it. And why should they? Who was I? I was his niece-in-law, or something, someone. I was no one, I did not matter, I had no grounds to miss him. Eventually, I was left with the odd prospect of grow-ing older than he had ever been, and a longing to meet him occasionally for lunch. Gradually I realized that it was this that he should have been to me: someone with whom I could have lunched; or not simply some*one*, he should have been my lunch date throughout my life. We would have met regularly to chew the cud (*upmarket* cud, of course).

Then, one day, years later, when I was nearly as old as he had ever been, I walked through Piccadilly on my way home from the National Portrait Gallery, dropped into Boots to buy throat pastilles, and saw him.

'*Goodness*,' he exclaimed.

I said, 'What are you doing here?' That was all, these were the only words that came, this was exactly what I needed to know: *what was he doing here?* What I noticed was that his face was unscarred: that face, which had always been too good to be true, now seemed even better.

I heard the woman on the till say, 'Forty-five, please,' and, 'do you need a bag?'

'No,' I replied, but without turning towards her. Then I

remembered to add, 'Thanks,' and to force a smile, but unfortunately I forgot to turn to face her. The coins went from my hand, the packet of pastilles returned, but my gaze never moved from Uncle Robbie. His eyes, mouth, hair, hairline: a photofit in which, for once, at last, everything fitted perfectly. No, there *was* a scar; but there had always been this scar, tiny and faint, close to one eye, a detail which I had forgotten, which I had never remembered. The scar twinkled in his pink skin, then the photofit slipped into a smile. Something which never comes with a photofit: a real, live smile. He continued, 'Haven't you grown!' Typical Uncle Robbie.

I demanded, '*What are you doing here?*'

And then he announced, 'Well, I'd like to take you to lunch.'

I followed him onto the street. Followed the precision haircut. The dull-ditchwater sheen of his raincoat, the very colour of confidence, quiet confidence, old money. In the open air, I could not see the whole of him: my eyes scrimped, as if I was trying to look into the sun and they were trying to save me. But I was no more confounded than when I had been told that he had died. What was odd was to have seen him in Boots in Piccadilly, but this had nothing to do with his supposed death, this would have been just as odd if he were alive. Because he was Kensington, through and through. I did not think that he was alive, but I did not know what to think. For a moment, following him through the shoppers, I wondered if *I* had died. What is the phrase, *Died and gone to Heaven? I-thought-I'd-died-and-gone-to-Heaven.* But then we reached the street and I knew that this was not Heaven because this was Piccadilly, and Piccadilly is not Heaven, not by any stretch of the imagination, anyone's imagination, believer or non-believer.

So I asked him, 'What were you doing in there?'

I was talking to the high collar, before he turned around. His shrug was stiff, because his hands were deep in his pockets. But the smile was loose, loopy, was definitely his smile.

'Waiting for you,' he replied.

'No, what were you doing *in there*?'

He reiterated, '*Waiting, for, you*,' and exhaled exasperation, *I mean*, 'you *were in there*, weren't you?'

'Yes,' of course, 'but . . .' but how to explain? '. . . that was just fate.'

He raised an eyebrow, for some reason.

And for some reason I flinched, and hurried, 'What I mean is that I'm not *usually* in there; I don't think that I've *ever* been in there, before today.'

'Well,' he concluded, lightly, pleasantly, quickly, 'that makes two of us,' before checking, 'how's the old throat?'

'Fine,' I replied on cue, before my whole body frowned with suspicion. 'How do you know about my throat?'

He paused for long enough and raised enough eyebrow to imply, *paranoid?* Then he nodded towards one of my pockets. 'Your purchase.'

'Oh.' My hands slunk into my pockets, one hand squeezed the packet, and my shoulders rose and clenched into a small shrug.

'I do hope that you don't mind about this.'

'*Mind?*' I could have chosen many words for how I was feeling, but *mind* was not one of them.

'But I couldn't wait any longer.' He smiled, briefly, slightly, ruefully.

I surprised myself by saying simply, 'You waited seven

years.' And I had not had to think; the date had grown with me like a pin in a bone.

He chose not to respond to this, glossed over this with a nod towards the shop. 'In there, I wasn't entirely truthful with you, I'm afraid. Because although I'd like nothing better, lunch is impossible.'

Why? And an answer washed through me: *fallen-on-hard-times*. But what was I saying? He was supposed to be *dead*: hard to imagine harder times. 'That's okay,' I hurried, 'we can walk in the park.'

'Ah, yes,' he murmured, appreciatively, 'the park, excellent,' before he turned and wobbled from the kerb into the path of the traffic.

In the same second, my hand went for him and he stepped back up to safety. My hand stayed in the air; my hand had gone to him but gone through him. So then I knew.

When he was back beside me, and when my breath was back, I dared to ask, 'Would you have been hurt?'

He smiled his sinking smile and ran a hand up through his hair.

I watched the hair shift and settle; shivered to realize that this was something that my own hand could not do.

'No,' he replied, 'I'm quite beyond hurt, but . . .', his gaze sloshed around the crowds, '. . . it's important to keep up appearances.'

I ventured, 'And is that why. . . ?'

He understood, smiled down onto me, confirmed, 'Yes: I am no longer so constituted as to be able to partake of lunch, shall we say.'

As *he* would say; as only Uncle Robbie would say.

Unfortunately, I was not so constituted, and I was starving.

So, I went back into Boots to buy a sandwich. This time, he waited on the street, and I watched him. He looked oddly uncomfortable for someone in such a comfortable coat. But I turned a blind eye and hurried back, already munching, sparky with blood sugar and bouncy with the fierce bubbling in my heart, to joke, 'I'd kiss your cheek, if I could.'

He made a show of recoiling: 'Ugh! – mayo mouth.'

'*Mayo mouth?*' This, from Uncle Robbie, and when he had been in purgatory for the last seven years?

We met regularly throughout the summer, always on Wednesdays and always in the park. I did not know where he had been, where he had come from, or where he went for the rest of the week, and for some reason I did not dare to ask. Which was not so very different from when he had been alive. I suppose that I did not dare to risk breaking the spell.

On the first few occasions, I forgot about food and was faint, fuzzy-headed, for much of the time. Eventually I learned to eat before I went to see him: surreptitious take-away pastries in Pall Mall.

The summer was soggy, nothing like a summer, but I barely noticed. Because I was happy. Because I had Uncle Robbie. I would have been even happier if I could have had his raincoat; but the raincoat, like lunch, was impossible. The park, in bad weather, was perfect for us: people passed through at quite a pace, wrapped in their dowdy coats, their eyes the colour of the sky, and they seemed oblivious to us. But perhaps no one looks at anyone else in London, not really, and not even in the parks. Perhaps especially not in the parks.

What did we talk about, during those afternoons? I soon learned that the simplest questions were the most difficult:

How are you? How have you been? I had no notion of his life, if he even had a life. And I assumed that he would know nothing of mine or anyone else's, so gossip would have been one-sided and no fun. But the big topics were better: we caught up on seven years of abstraction, of arts and politics, making up for the seven lost years of chatter that had been the ingredient missing from the lunches of my late twenties.

But I was thirty-one. I had begun to live alone, having split up with my lover of many years. The timing of the split was odd, out of sync with the bust-ups of our friends, coming years behind the first wave of youthful mistakes and years before the mid-life crises. At this time, I did not seem to see my friends except for dinner in their homes. To me, when I had been a few years younger, to be grown-up was to have dinners with bottles of wine effortlessly produced from racks, to have real coffee, and central heating, and central heating *on*, *and* an open fire in a surround of original tiles. I had mistaken grown-up for middle class, but, in any case, I had become both, I had *arrived*, so why did I sometimes feel that I had crash-landed? Whenever I tried to talk to my friends, their noses were in wine glasses or wine guides, and the conversation was obliterated by the grinding of coffee beans. We were in the late eighties and their talk was of shares, which were anything but. There was a sprinkling of children, too, which seemed to eclipse whole lives.

So I told no one about Uncle Robbie, but not simply because there was no one to tell. I filled with my secret and the overspill became a docile little shadow, a comfort to me. With so much secrecy, I developed a slippery smile, dropping unspoken hints from the corners of my mouth as if I had had a stroke. Which, I suppose, in a sense, I had: a stroke of luck. A stroke which cut me loose from the ordinary, everyday world. I spent the days waiting for darkness, for sleep, when I could be alone with my secret. The moment I woke, every day, I knew that something was different, that I knew something that no one else knew, that I was living something that no one else was living. Which is exactly what love or the death of a loved one will do, and in my case I was living a unique combination.

Whenever I met up with him, I had a desire to explore London, to retrace footsteps that I was not quite sure I had ever taken: from landmark to landmark – the Tower, Monument, Big Ben, the Drury Lane Ghost, or Dick Whittington's cat, and the man in Petticoat Lane who made a living from selling photos to people who had posed with his two tiny monkeys which were dressed as babies. I could not quite tell if these were my own memories: my family had been a London family, with a London house. Then Grandpa had died and Grandma sold up, moved out, pensioned herself off to a bungalow in the country and sent us to the suburbs. London had been denied me. Or, London *as home* had been denied me: grown-up, I rented. I had grown up in a family that had remained oriented towards London: *Town* meant London. My father commuted, often came home late complaining of *a body on the line*. He blamed Grandma for losing London for us, or for losing the money that would have come into the family if she had waited for property prices to rocket; and she blamed Grandpa, but for dying: a chain of blame, one of our stronger family ties.

But I could not explore London with Uncle Robbie, because

he did not like crowds: he was afraid of *not* bumping into people. But once, buoyed up, on my way home, I detoured to my family's old house. After a search, I found it, but it seemed to have shrunk, and in an upstairs window stood a man with a mobile phone. The rooms were stocked with distressed pine: apt words for my own feelings, on the journey back to my little flat. The following week, I tried in vain to interest Uncle Robbie in a trip to St Paul's, where, as far as I could remember, I had never been. Where, as far as I was concerned, I *should* have been.

'*Ah*,' he enthused, '"Tuppence a bag."'

I said, 'What?'

'"Tuppence a bag."'

Suddenly I remembered, sang, '"*Feed the birds*. . ."?'

And he smiled, *Yes*.

I said, 'At primary school, one of my favourite songs was "*La Cucaracha*", which I never knew meant *cockroach*. How could anyone compose such a jolly song about a *cockroach*?'

The smile expanded, somehow, to include his eyebrows. 'Well, I suppose that you could say, If-you-can't-beat-'em, sing-a-song-about-'em.'

But I was doubtful: 'You *could* . . .'

Then I remembered, '"John Brown's body lies a-mouldering in the grave", can you *believe* that we would gather around the piano with our tambourines and triangles to sing *that*?'

He laughed, 'And I *bet* that none of you knew who John Brown was,' before adding, 'and *Dixie*.'

'What?'

'*Dixie*: yet more Confederacy mysteriously misplaced in British schools.'

I frowned.

So he frowned. 'You never had music lessons?'

'No,' but now I was remembering, 'our other favourite was "My bonnie lies over the ocean" which I thought was "My *body* lies over the ocean", which never made much sense.'

He said, 'No.' Then, '"Like a patient etherised upon a table."'

Fairly seriously, I reminded him, 'I'm not seventeen, I don't need our conversation to be littered with literary references.'

And he ruffled my hair. Or perhaps the breeze ruffled my hair.

I said, 'Do you know what I *really* remember when I think of primary school?'

'No?'

I was not quite sure if he or his smile had spoken.

'Apollo 11, which happened when I was leaving primary school, leaving for good, moving on to secondary. Those men were going to the moon, and I was going to secondary school: everything was changing, everyone was moving on. Except for my grandpa, I suppose, because he was in the Whittington for the last time, and I went to watch the moon landing with him, on the telly in the day room. He was thrilled, he told me that we were watching the future. But what was wrong with televisions, in those days? Because the astronauts looked like ghosts, do you remember? They were moving around but they were see-through.'

Very quietly, he was exclaiming, '*Goodness*, aren't you *young*.'

'No,' I said, looking away over the drab park, 'not any more.'

* * *

149

Around this time, I began to see more of Helen, of whom, in the past few years, in the way of the world, I had seen very little. My visits became more frequent, but carefully low-key so that she would not notice. Not that she was the noticing kind; noticing was not her strong point. She had two small sons, by then, and seemed to work by instinct: she climbed the stairs to comfort the children before I had detected their cries, she ran baths before they were dirty and cooked meals for the moment when they complained of hunger. She was married to the boys' father: *a boring bastard*, she would say, almost fondly, but wistfully because only the *boring* was apposite. He drove a bulky BMW, and spent the weekends driving around the country to displays and parades of old-fashioned fire-engines: *fire-engines with no cutting equipment*, she had explained to me, contemptuously.

One day, I managed the question that I had been longing to ask her: 'Do you ever think of Uncle Robbie?'

Was he still *Uncle* Robbie? To him, so far, I had avoided any form of address.

'Oh, *yes*.' Her face became misty, and not simply with a sigh of cigarette smoke. We were sitting on spindly stools at the breakfast bar which she kept in her house when everyone else had converted to old pine tables. Her hem was high and sharp on her thighs, and there were dimples on the thighs which had nothing to do with youth. She began to talk about Uncle Robbie as if he had been an old drinking partner (which was, in a sense, I suppose, exactly what he had been): no real *talk*, nothing specific, but lots of appreciative murmurs, the verbal equivalent of back-slapping. Not for the first time, I wondered whether she had that lack of memory common to people who care for small children, who are required to live in an excess of the present. As she talked, or murmured and sighed, she dropped ash, which was how she had survived ever since she had ceased to be an old soak: by relying upon smoke and ash to take the edge off the world.

What I loved about Helen was the scent of her that survived the smell of cigarettes: a scent which women are not supposed to have; or, perhaps, *the* scent which women *are* supposed to have, but are not bold enough to wear and choose to wipe away. She smelled ripe, both sweet and musty, sweet but on the turn: old sweat and babies, even though her babies were grown. In her younger days, in the days of Uncle Robbie, I had heard her refer to herself as *a strictly soap-and-water girl*, but now she did not even seem to bother with the soap. There was something else that I loved: the black which rose in her to darken the rings around her eyes, to silt under her nails and in their cuticles, to fatten her moles and display the natural colour of her dyed and nicotine-stained hair. These were glorious imperfections, adding to the rich patina of bruising left by the rough-and-tumble of the little boys. Each time I went to see her, I was struck by her faded grandeur; although, in a sense, there was nothing *faded* about her, she was *extravagantly* flawed.

My mother liked to refer to Helen's appearance as *the love-me-or-leave-me look*. But I knew where my heart lay. And, anyway, no one had ever left Helen. If my father attempted defence by saying, *Helen has kept her looks*, my mother would laugh, *Kept them where?* Then he countered, *There's nothing so unattractive in a woman as bitchiness.* The problem between my parents was simple but serious: my mother was hardening with age, but my father was softening. Helen was oblivious. Having no vanity to trip her up, to lay her low, she was a survivor. My parents had always complained that *Helen doesn't care*; but the only person about whom Helen did not care was herself.

'He'd love the boys,' she said, suddenly. Then, 'And they are his, in a way.'

I tottered on my stool. 'What do you mean?'

'I mean . . . I mean . . .' she shrugged, chucking ash, 'I mean, he made me who I am, and now I'm making them who they are.'

I came to her because I needed to know if she ever thought of Uncle Robbie, and what she thought of him, but also because I wanted to replace his photo. Her photo. Of him. The photo that I had taken from a pile in her house sometime in the year following his death. *Borrowed*, rather than taken. Not that she would have noticed. Not that he was even looking into the camera. The photo that, for weeks, I had been carrying in my bag between my home and hers. But now, suddenly, I wanted to hold onto it, *for dear life*: rigid on that ridiculous stool, I tried to quell my fear that the little boys would come downstairs for their ritual rummage in *Auntie-Miranda's-bag* and would come across my booty.

A week later, when I met Uncle Robbie, I mentioned Helen. Which was my first mention of her, to him. 'I saw Helen, this week.'

'Ah, *Tink*,' he enthused. 'How *is* she?'

Rain was clattering all around us onto leaves, onto a parkload of leaves. I had remembered to bring an umbrella, beneath which I stood alone but nevertheless wetter than him. 'She thinks you'd love the boys, her two little boys.'

'Oh, I do, I do,' the same tone.

I tipped up my umbrella, to follow his eyes. 'You do?'

'I do,' he echoed, smiling over the park. The smile was for no one I could see. From where I was standing, I looked up into and through his eyes. Not very different from looking down into clean sunny water: the bottom everywhere, in suspension.

'But how do you know them?'

'Well . . .' he seemed surprised by my question, he seemed not to know, 'well, I *can see*.'

My body crackled with shock, with the hundreds of implications, the chief of which was that he must have been able to see me, too, over the years. But for now, all that I needed to know was, 'Do you, have you ever . . .' *how to ask?* '. . . have you ever been in parks with anyone else?' I added a pathetic, euphemistic, 'In recent years?'

'No,' he said, so forcefully that the word tore like a plea.

I held harder onto the stem of my umbrella, which shook above me and dropped rain. 'Not even with Helen?' I dared, but timidly. 'Or . . .' I had never spoken the name of the woman who had eventually followed Helen, I had never even *thought* her name, 'Lorna?'

'Listen,' he emphasized, 'they're my past, but you're my future; only you are my future.' He laid his hands on my shoulders, and I was certain that I detected his touch. 'Do you understand?' he implored.

'Yes,' I said, because I loved him, but this was the first real lie.

My lie shut me up for a while, for our walk back to the road. For weeks, I had been holding back my questions for the time when I would feel closer to him. But six weeks had passed, and I was no closer.

When we came to the end of the path, he said, cheerfully, 'You're my second chance, my last chance.'

I did not know what I felt. Until I remembered an old word, an old favourite, which had come with me from childhood into adolescence with an appropriate slip in meaning: *spooked*.

He was saying, 'Same time, same place?'

Which was hardly a question, because I would hardly say no.

But, 'No,' he said, suddenly, 'same time, in your favourite bookshop.'

Before I could ask him how he knew which bookshop was my favourite, he smiled and disappeared. He *disappeared*, which he had never done before, to me. Or not that I had noticed. But perhaps, until then, I had been too happy to look behind me, or not for long enough, or far enough, or hard enough.

The following week, I found him by *Languages*, scanning the shelves.

As I approached him, he pointed to one of the books: 'Absolutely fascinating, don't you think?' It was a book of Japanese lessons, *Minimum Essential Politeness*. 'Do you think that you could possibly hold the book for me, and turn over a page or two? And then, perhaps, with your help, I could cover a lesson each week.'

I laughed, boisterously, probably impolitely. '*Japanese?* I can't imagine anything less *you*.'

Chivalrously, he echoed with his own laugh, but one which was less convincing, less sure, slightly slow and broken.

'Ah, but, well,' he explained, bashfully, 'Japanese is the language of the future.'

'Yes, but you don't *have* a future,' my words skidded from me; I had been thinking them, and then suddenly they were real, spoken.

He looked at me. Or perhaps he was already looking, but he stayed looking; his eyes stayed still. Which was a look that I had never seen from him. *Careful.* Neither of us moved, nor breathed. We waited for the moment to settle, to die away. Then one of us – I thought that it was him, but it must have been me – folded my hair behind my ear, and I stood exposed, chastened.

'How very right you are,' he said: a sonorous murmur, like something spoken to reassure a child.

What I did not know was if I had inadvertently hit on the truth, like a child.

I followed him from the shop, bumping into people and chanting a mantra of apology. A bookshop is not an easy shop to leave in a hurry: the customers positioned singly and still, and bowed in contemplation, like anglers. Dodging them, I shook with the bass-beat from my furious heart. Because if he was not there when I reached the pavement, there was nowhere for me to look for him. As I passed people, I wanted to yell into their closed-down book-focused faces, *This is a matter of life and death.* And then, pushing through the doorway, I saw that he was there, looking upwards into a sky sliced of horizon and shrunk to inky thumbprints on a backdrop.

When he sensed that I had joined him, he announced his change of subject: 'I'd love to spend some time with you away from London,' he mused, breezily, 'but unfortunately I have no car.'

I swooped low to try to catch my breath.

Above me, he continued to muse: 'I wonder if I still have a *licence*.'

'*Robbie*,' I shouted, snapping upright, '*why* did you drive into that tanker?'

His face was luminous and slack with shock. 'I hope that you don't mind me saying,' he began to recover himself, his voice remaining faint, 'but I'm not sure that it's really a question of *why*.'

He was right, of course: this was not the question, merely a wail. The real question was: '*Why* did you not *think*?'

He had no answer for me; his mouth opened and closed, and his eyes went somewhere else, anywhere else.

'Had you been drinking?' Because he had died in the old days, when people drank and drove.

'*No* . . .'

'Why did you not *brake*?' My shriek was muffled by the wobbly throb of a stationary bus.

'I did brake, that was the problem,' and he appealed, 'you *know* that was the problem.'

'Less *hard*, then.'

He dropped back, announced to no one, 'This is ridiculous,' before straightening to insist, 'if I had braked less hard, I would have *definitely* hit the tanker.'

'Oh, so,' I had lost control, 'the hit that you *did* achieve did *not* qualify as *definite*?'

He despaired audibly, looked down to the pavement.

And I cried up into the sky, 'Why did it *rain*?'

Quietly, he dismissed this: 'There is always rain somewhere; one has to learn to live with rain.'

I was crying, but his face seemed more pained. My face

felt cool, calm, nothing but a wash of tears. His hands were high and cramped to match his expression; they hovered helplessly over my shoulders, then dropped down but fell through me.

He said, 'I made a mistake, a momentary mistake; a miscalculation.'

Were we referring to the same accident? Were we speaking the same language? I did not know how to make him see.

Fiercely, I told him, 'But that's the kind of miscalculation that you *simply do not make*.' Then I cried, 'Did you not think *of us*?' Of whom? Me, Helen, perhaps even the Lorna-person, and Helen's children, and even, one day, my own children: all of us, *the living*, a party-load of guests who had been dumped by our host.

Defensively, he explained, 'I wasn't thinking, I was driving; and you know very well that whatever anyone says, however hard one tries, there's a difference.'

I continued, 'Why were you driving *so fast*?'

'I always *did*, that was what I *did*.' And then he admitted, 'I don't know.'

'And why did you wait seven years to come back?' Which, for seven weeks, was all that I had really wanted to ask.

He had an answer. 'I couldn't have come any earlier, because you had to do your mourning, you had to have done your mourning.'

'*Oh*,' I piped sarcasm through my tears, 'and do I seem to have succeeded?'

He admitted, 'I had no idea.'

'Perhaps you don't know as much as you think that you know.' But I was not telling him the whole truth, which was that *I* had had no idea, that these tears were a surprise to me, too.

His eyes came back to mine, and he offered, tentatively, 'But, then, I was never much good at knowing when people were angry with me.'

He had avoided saying *women*: I smiled, in spite of myself. 'But you could have come sooner: I was over you – as much as I was ever going to be over you – in a year or so.' For some reason, suddenly, I was almost laughing: 'So why *seven*?'

He shrugged, 'I was late?'

And I did laugh, a little.

But then, foolishly, he told me his other reason: 'You were in a relationship.'

I stiffened, self-conscious but also suspicious. 'So?'

'So,' he emphasized, patiently, 'I had to wait.'

I waited for an explanation.

'Oh, come on,' he hurried, '*think*: think of the secrecy involved in this; I could never have come back when you were involved with someone.'

I bit slowly into my lip, not to clamp shut my mouth but to try to prompt some words.

'For me,' he explained, 'you were dangerously close to someone else.'

My words, when they came to me, seemed to be the only words that I had ever had. Any other words which I had ever spoken had been utterly unimportant. 'I loved you *so* much.'

He was flapping, blinking, coughing, treating this as inconsequential: 'I know, I knew.'

'Actually, no,' I contemplated, 'I don't think that you *did* know. Because if you'd have known, then you would never have died.'

Flustered, he countered, 'Oh, *really . . .*'

I shrugged, but did not lower my arms, folded them instead around my body. 'I happen to think that it's true: you would never knowingly have hurt me so much.'

He tried, 'Hitting the tanker was not something that I *did*.'

I muttered, 'Just obeying orders from testosterone?'

'Was not something that I did *to you*, the world does not revolve *around you*,' although this was said kindly.

I explained, 'You would have taken more care.' I wanted to complain, *Do women go around driving into tankers?*

'Well, anyway,' he smiled, hopefully, 'I'm here now.'

And this struck me as irrevocably male: the mindless expectation of forgiveness. And it was untrue: 'Are you?' I taunted, and swiped my hand through him.

He shrank from me, a spasm of fear.

I walked away.

'Next week?' he called.

'Maybe.'

'*Miranda . . .*'

Turning briefly, I reminded him, '*Maybe*, but how do I know? Remember: the world doesn't revolve around you.'

But, of course, I worried all week: would he be there, when I went back? I had learned that my love for him had not stopped when he had died, nor when he had come back and we had had a row: the *love* would have to *die*. And my love for him was alive and kicking. When I returned to the park, after a very long week, he was there. But we did not stroll, we stayed beneath some trees and paced fitfully, circling each other.

I worked my way through a bar of Fry's Chocolate Cream,

with which I had come prepared. This is something which I do, very occasionally, when I am nervous. A habit which has something to do with the tidy snap of the black chocolate and the sticky burn of the fondant on the roof of my mouth.

I barely looked at him whilst he spoke. His statement took the usual format. He began, 'I've been thinking,' and continued with the expected, 'this is not going to work.'

I shrugged, snapped, bit into a solid corner, and smoothed the crumpled silver wrapper. I knew that this was the truth, I would allow this; but I did not want to have to say it or to take any part in it.

He said, 'You have your own life.'

I had no argument with this. I frowned down into the tiny sheet of silver foil.

He continued, 'I love you, but we live in different worlds.'

Tingling with the *love you*, I could suffer the *different worlds*.

'This is an unnatural state of affairs for a young woman.'

I was suddenly bitter, 'Oh, and you'd know, would you? You'd know all about natural states of affairs for young women?'

Was I still too young to know that anger has life, but bitterness kills? I looked up to see that he was giving me what is termed, for some reason, a long look, which became the longest look that I had ever seen until I realized that I had lost sight of him altogether. Too late: he was gone.

I went nowhere for a long time. And when I eased up and moved off, the chocolate bar had become a marbled silver ball in the palm of my hand. I knew, simply knew, that he had gone for good. (Why gone *for good*? Is there no equivalent for dire situations?) Yet, the following week, I went along – same time, same place – to check.

I waited for forty minutes, standing my ground but sitting on a bench, before I gave up, walked up into town. In Leicester Square, passing the cinemas, I saw that *Peter Pan* was having a revival. My favourite film when I was a child. But why? Peter? Or Wendy? The flying, or the pirates? Neverland? Odd how, to children, the everyday world is not the normal world, how the make-believe world is more real. Or perhaps not odd, because how normal, really, is the everyday world, to a child? I remembered that the pirates had been very important to me. Why? The violent expropriation? The life at sea? I had never had much regard for land, for landing, for being grounded, for proper grounds. And then I remembered the lost boys, and wondered why there were no lost *girls*? And knew why: because everyone loves little boys, innocent little bunglers, but girls are never wholly children, they are old before their years. In the days of *Peter Pan*, in the real, everyday days, lost girls would have worked the streets, would have been pregnant.

Pregnant. This was when I realized: I realized that I had lost track of time; that I was late, that I had missed a period. I had been thinking of nothing but Wednesdays, I had been living for Wednesdays. Pregnancy was possible: my previous relationship had come to an amicable end, and, possibly, during one of our inevitable goodbye sessions, frivolous with the prospect of imminent freedom, I had worn my cap rather too jauntily. *A mistake, a miscalculation.* Then and there, I walked to the Boots in Piccadilly and bought a pregnancy testing kit.

I did not want a baby, there was no room in my life for a

baby, my life was already a tight fit. In Boots, when the woman asked me if I wanted a bag, I had to stop myself from replying, *Yes, plastic, please, for my face.* Cradling my purchase, I took a bus to the station and followed the sign for *Ladies.* Paid my twenty pence and used the facilities to the full. Because I had to know, I could not do anything, or go anywhere, even to my own home, until I knew: if I was pregnant, then the world was a different place and I was a different person. Time stopped still, although hundreds of women came and went. And then, seemingly in no time at all, the kit held the answer: blue, Madonna blue, to tell me that if everything went well, I was going to have a baby.

If everything *went well?* I stood amongst all those women, most of whom must have had this same result at some time or other during their lives, but they came and went on their journeys and I was utterly alone. With a baby. *My* baby. Another life that I was going to have to do on my own. Had Uncle Robbie known? When I leaned onto a basin and looked into the mirror, I could see: I was puffy, shiny, and buxom; I *had* grown. He *had known*, I was sure. And had *I* known? I think that I had been about to know, when I bumped into Uncle Robbie: because why else, utterly out of character, had I decided to buy pastilles rather than aspirin? My body had known, but Uncle Robbie had distracted me. He had given me time. Made me happy. Given me time to be happy. Then I knew that I had to hold onto this baby: I had had enough loss, there was no time for more.

When I left the *Ladies,* I crossed the concourse to buy a drink, and the boy behind the counter said to me, 'Coffee, large, with a small cream.'

I said, 'Who asked *you?*'

'Well,' he became flustered, his hand went to rake his hair but hit his chef's hat, '*you usually* do, around this time on Wednesdays.'

I had never seen him before, or not that I knew. I scanned the menu above him, and then pronounced, frostily, '*Mineral water*, please.'

He obeyed, but, opening the bottle, checked with me, 'You okay?'

I said, '*Ice*, please.'

He looked up from the ice bucket, but said nothing.

'And a salad sandwich, please. No egg, no cheese,' nothing to run poison into my taken-over body, down the cord into my baby.

He placed a package of sandwich next to the bottle on the Perspex counter. '*Bag?*'

I flinched. 'Yes, plastic, please, for my face.' Had I spoken aloud? Startled, I glanced into his eyes to check. They were the colour of Fry's Chocolate Cream, the chocolate and the fondant.

He leaned over the counter and said, 'Let me tell you something: this is my summer job, I'm serving here and trying to read the odd textbook on International Relations, I don't know which is more boring but both have to be done, and every Wednesday afternoon you come along for your large coffee and small cream and you're the happiest person that I've seen for seven days. But today, no. So, has something happened?'

I had always wondered, 'What *is* International Relations?'

He wondered, '*Are?*' but then decided, 'never mind.'

So I told him, 'Someone has left me, but someone else has joined me. It's the old, sad story: I'm pregnant. Without a paddle.' As I spoke, I slid a straw from the box.

'*Pregnant,*' he enthused. 'Oh, *wow.*'

Wow? This was not quite what I had expected. I looked up, sharply, straw drawn, to see that he was looking at me as if pregnancy had never happened to anyone before; and I was going to say so, to say, *It's not as if this has never happened to anyone before, you know.* But then I was struck that perhaps this had never happened to *him* before, and certainly had never happened to *me.* This was new for both of us.

Reader, I had his children. Not for a few years, of course: I had my own child, and then his, two of them. Not that anyone has ever made the distinction: we all know, but we live our lives regardless. This evening, Christmas Eve, I was driving home with all three of them from Helen's house in London. I had taken the girls with me to fetch my eldest, who had been staying there for a few days, which seems to be his new hobby. Of course, he had wanted to come home on his own, in his own time; but I had wanted to drop in on Helen, who, in the Christmas chaos, I had not seen for nearly three weeks.

We had hijacked his trip, and he was suitably resentful: on the way home, in the darkness of the passenger seat, he was all slumped shoulders, brows, and lower lip. Whenever I glanced over, I had to resist an urge to push the hair away from his eyes, the non-verbal version of *Sit up straight.* He is fifteen, and spends most of his time in his black-painted bedroom which is hung with Catholic iconography (he tells me, *You underestimate the importance of ritual*). Glancing over to my shadowy son, I lapsed back into my worry that I was losing him. Wondered when I had last seen a smile from him. He has a crush on Helen, though. Not that he would call – or even think of – his fascination as a crush. Because, after all, Helen is fifty-three: a kittenish fifty-three, but fifty-three nevertheless. And not that he smiles at *her*. But *crush* depicts the way that his eyes follow her, unblinkingly, although whenever she turns to him, he can do nothing but blink. And why else did he refer to her kaftan as a *gown*? But fair enough: he stays with Helen because she lives in London, and for the company of her boys, too.

We were a few streets away from home when I glanced over again and checked the mirror to discover that the only one of them who was awake was the dog: our eyes met on the mirror in a frank exchange of boredom. I was driving slowly, struggling to keep the speed limit, because the only cars that I had seen for a while were police cars. Because people leave here for Christmas, to slot back into normal families: our town has a big population of young people, with some retired people who made the mistaken assumption that this town is the same as others on the South Coast. Here, almost everyone lives singly or in couples, in the flats which have annexed the Victorian downtown and the thirties rim, both of which were built by fresh-air fanatics who overlooked the fact that half of the space, and thus half of the air, is taken by the sea. When I explained this to my son, once, to help him with his geography homework, with *catchment areas* and *distribution of industry*, he looked at my diagram, a semicircle, and laughed, 'Oh, yes: now that I *see*, it's *obvious*.'

Which made me laugh: 'Ah, yes, but isn't everything obvious when you see? Isn't that what seeing *is*?'

Some families do live here, in houses, and, all year round, we put on a brave show: we do the usual things, patronize a particular school and a piano teacher. I began to drive the circumference of the park, and had a vision of summer, memories of strolls in shorts, of flower-fluffy shrubberies, of trays of teacups borne from the café onto the vine-canopied terrace: a different world, but one which will come again and again and again. Even if nowadays the days seem dark despite sunrise, and the world is wringing wet whether or not there has been rain. Whoever decided that Hell was *hot*?

Suddenly, my elder daughter said, 'Mrs Sims –' her teacher '– told us that the most important bit of last century was the man on the moon.'

And the little one, apparently woken, exclaimed, 'I can *see* him. *Look*.'

I heard her sister mutter, '*Stupid*.'

Switching my eyes from the full moon to the mirror, I explained, 'No, that's the man *in* the moon,' adding hurriedly, 'well, not really,' before continuing, 'the man *on* the moon was a real man, some real men who went into space in a rocket and landed on the moon.'

The question piped behind me: 'Why?'

I had to admit, 'I don't know,' but tried, 'just to see, I suppose.'

'To see what?'

True, 'I don't know.'

My elder daughter wanted to know, 'Do you remember the man on the moon?'

An opportunity for a little test: 'Date?'

My son growled, 'Fifties. Had to be.'

In a sense, he was right: in a sense, the moon landing *had to* have been in the fifties; if I had had to go for an intelligent guess, I would have said the fifties. But I had to correct him.

'1969,' and then, 'yes, I remember.'

Now she wanted to know, 'So, was the man on the moon the most important thing in *your* life, Mum?'

From our previous conversations, I know that, in her view, the twentieth century means my life. I tried to explain, 'Well, no, I wouldn't say so; not really; that's not really how life is.'

'So, what *was* the most important thing?'

I was thinking, hard. 'In *my* life?' Then I knew: 'When my Uncle Robbie died.' This was when I remembered him. I had not thought of him for years.

One of the girls asked, 'Who was your Uncle Robbie?'

'Auntie Helen's first husband.'

A shriek: 'She had a husband *before Uncle Graham*?'

Apparently amused, my son exclaimed in a whisper, '*Jesus*.' Then asked me, 'Was he as bad as Graham?'

I laughed, '*Oh* no,' checked, 'but did you not know?'

An indignant voice from behind me: 'You never *said*.'

'I didn't?' I could hardly believe that. 'I did. But you didn't listen; you kids *never* listen.'

'Before we were born?'

'Yes.'

The little one said, '*Grandma* says.'

Suddenly I was curious: 'Says what?'

'Says *about him*, sometimes.'

The older one insisted, 'She does *not*, *I've* never heard her.'

'Says *what* about him?'

She pondered. 'Says that he cut a dash.'

I smiled, nowhere, towards the moon. 'Well, yes, he did.'

Then she asked. 'What does that mean?'

And I could not explain.

So I simply continued, 'When I lost my Uncle Robbie, I realized . . .'

But now, typically, my son wanted to know, 'How did he die?'

'Car crash.' Tactlessly, I added, 'He taught me to drive, you know.'

The slumped shadow swelled and made a show of feeling for the door handle. 'I'll walk, I could do with the exercise.'

'Oh ha *ha*.' But then I thought to whisper, 'Don't panic your sisters.'

One of whom was asking, 'Was no one *else* important when they died, then?'

Good question. I tried to think, explain: 'Well, he was the first; the first is the most important.'

I swear that I saw my son smirk; and he refolded his arms. But then, suddenly serious, he asked, 'What did you realize?'

'What did I realize?'

'You said that when you lost him, you *realized* . . .'

'*Oh*.' But what *had* I realized? 'I realized . . .' Then I found that I was saying, 'There was a lot of talk from the men on the moon about how, when they had looked back down to earth, they realized . . . oh, you know, our world is so small but it's all that we have, that kind of stuff, the obvious kind of stuff.' I glanced over to him. As ever, he was looking out of the window. No response, but his silence was different from before, was dense with his expectation. So, I had to continue. 'Once, on telly, I heard Neil Armstrong say that when they were coming back down, there was so much to do, but that if he could have the time again, he would want to spend it simply looking out of the window.'

The silence wanted to know, *Yes*, and, *so?*

'When Uncle Robbie . . .' *came back?* 'Well, I was not quite here, and I was taking time to look out of the window.'

Nothing, for a moment, before a growl, which came sliding on sarcasm: 'Yeah, right.' *Too much brandy in your brandy butter, Mother.*

I was certain that I had lost him. But then he smiled, slowly, briefly. And I knew that I was wrong about losing him, because however solitary or secretive or broken, his smile has always spelled, *Yeah, right, I'm with you.*

8

A GOOD AIRING

'Get *dressed*,' Mum whines at me, on her way through the kitchen.

'It's too hot.' Ten o'clock in the morning and too hot for clothes. And, anyway, I *am* dressed, in a sense: I am wearing a big old shirt, which I bought at a jumble sale, whose label says *Savile Row*.

I pick a handful of cornflakes from the top of the packet.

'*Don't* do that, pour yourself a bowl.' She hurries into the hallway.

I slam the crackly wrapping back into the box.

'Eat *something*.' Do *something*, *anything*.

I sigh as loudly as possible. 'It's *too hot*.'

Her scowl has transferred to the mirror in the hallway. Her eyelids are furry with dark brown powder; hardly the natural look: they look like bruises. She dabs the tip of her little finger into her mouth and then brushes the spittle into the corner of one eye, replacing one smudge with another: a dark brown streak drifts towards the eyebrow. She mutters something and shuffles closer to the mirror, sliding forward on the wooden base of her Scholls.

'Are you coming?' she barks via the mirror.

'No. Where?'

'Church.'

'You must be joking.'

The chocolate-button pupils slide towards me. 'Am I laughing?'

Church: the School Leavers' Service, presumably; Georgia's leaving service. 'All Things Bright and Beautiful' and the gift of a dictionary from the Governors. It was the same for me; and, presumably, a couple of years later, it was the same for Vinnie, who has never shown much interest in his dictionary. And now Georgia's turn: poor Georgie-porgie, swapping Play-doh for PE, utterly unsuspecting.

'No,' I clarify, 'I'm not coming.'

Mum pouts into the mirror. She produces, apparently from nowhere, a nub of lipstick, and drags this around her lips. The nub is frosty pink; she is icing her lips. At school we coat our lips with chalk when we want to pretend that we have been sick so that we can be excused from PE.

'Georgia came to yours,' she says.

'Georgia was *five*, she was with you, she didn't have any *choice*.'

'Choice?' Mum's eyebrows flex into an arch of dismay. 'What choice do *I* have?'

I wish that I had never mentioned choice.

She deflates dramatically. 'Well, I suppose I'll just have to go on my own: yet another place that I'll have to go on my own.'

I wish that I was still in bed. I unscrew the lid from the jar of marmalade and reach inside with my fingernail to extract a strand of peel.

'You don't *have* to go.'

'Oh *no*,' she sings with sarcasm from the mirror.

I was only trying to help. But I know what she is trying to do: she is trying to imply that I do not understand the nuances of village life, that I am naïve, oblivious to obligation, unschooled in the ways of the world. But I do understand, and she does not have to go. Nobody goes.

'I've been invited,' she stresses, 'so I'll go.' *I've started, so I'll finish*.

Everyone is invited, and nobody goes. But I know what she will say if I say that nobody goes: *Mrs Simmons goes, and Mrs Darley, and Gemma's mother* ... A long list of locals. Then I would have to stop myself from saying, *See what I mean? – Nobodies*.

'Anyway,' she continues, 'I swapped my shift to a late, especially.'

Now she will say, *But I don't know why I bother* ...

On cue, she turns from the mirror with, 'But I don't know why I bother, because my efforts aren't appreciated.'

Unappreciated by me, she means, or Vinnie, or Georgia: *Ungrateful bloody kids*.

She swoops over the table, removing the cornflakes packet, jar of marmalade, loaf, butter, milk, which I would have done in time, in my own time.

'And Georgia insisted on wearing those dungarees again this morning (one day, I'm going to have to do something drastic about those dungarees). I said, *You can't wear those, PLEASE, GEORGIA, NOT to church*. And her *Ghostbusters* T-shirt.'

The cornflakes, marmalade, and loaf thud into the cupboard like skittles.

'What do you care?' I call to her over the noise, stretching from my chair into the crockery cupboard for a coffee cup. 'You're not religious.'

She snatches ahead of me into the cupboard, slams a coffee cup onto the table in front of me.

'Oh, I'm not worried that *God* will think badly of me; I'm worried about everyone else.'

She disappears again into the hallway. 'I'll be back around twelve.'

'Glad you told me: I'll see to the bunting.'

I hear a distant *tut*. And an even more distant, 'Lola!'

'What?'

'Can you come and fetch these things.'

What *things*?

'*Now*, please.'

I switch on the kettle and stride down the hallway towards the front door. Mum is outside, in the driveway, picking tea towels from a rhododendron bush.

'They've had a good airing,' she says, turning to me with the small pile.

Suddenly, behind her, the bush moves: our neighbour, Gordon, leaning over from his driveway. His smile is enthusiastic: those huge white teeth, that huge brown moustache. I have never seen him miserable; his face seems not to have been made for misery.

'Good morning, Mrs Judd; good morning, Lola.' He nods to each of us, two small bows. His hand, coming through the leaves, offers a small cactus. 'Cactus weather,' he says. 'And this one is spare.'

He is always giving us spares. The tea towel bush was spare.

He works with plants: outside and in, designing. He works from home, with a small van. From the doorstep, I can see the van, parked in his driveway: glossy racing green, painted with thick cream letters, *Brierly Landscapes*.

Mum looks down into his hand and says, 'Oh, thanks.' Hugging the tea towels, she nods in my direction.

I step down from the doorstep and reach for the little pot.

'Yes, thanks,' Mum says flatly to Gordon. 'It's lovely.'

It is a small hairy stump: the usual cactus.

Mum shuffles backwards and nudges me towards the porch.

'Are you going to the service?' Gordon asks.

She stops. 'Service?'

'Leavers' Service?'

'Oh, Leavers' Service, yes.'

'I do *love* Leavers' Service,' he enthuses, 'I think it's my favourite. I'm hoping to pop in.'

Gordon is leader of the choir. He conducts the Carol Service every year and takes the choir on tour to old folks' homes. He sings solo at weddings on Saturdays. He organizes the jumble sales and bazaars in aid of the church roof.

'Is Georgia leaving?'

'Yes.'

'Goodness, she's growing up,' he says appreciatively.

'Yes,' says Mum wistfully.

He turns to me. 'And has school finished for you, Lola? Exams over?'

'Yes.'

'And will you go back in the autumn?'

I shrug. 'Depends on my results.'

'Ah, yes. And what will you do, if you go back?'

'Don't know. Depends. French, perhaps. History.'

He nods thoughtfully. 'Well, if you need any work, we've been thinking of having some help in the house: nothing heavy, and of course we'll pay whatever you tell us is the going rate.' A deepening of the many creases of his smile.

But before I can say a word, Mum is telling him, 'Sorry,

Gordon, but I'll be keeping her *very* busy in *this* house over the summer.'

'Ah, well,' he nods towards my hands, the cactus, 'you like gardening?'

'If I know her,' Mum says, 'the only thing that she'll be planting in my garden this summer is herself, on *my* sun-lounger.'

We mumble and smile our goodbyes, and I follow Mum indoors, into the kitchen.

Frowning over the cactus, she decides, 'Dump that in the spice-rack for now.'

I am furious with her: 'Why did you tell Gordon that I'm busy? Why did you say that I couldn't work for him? You know I need the money.'

'It's not right,' she says, fussing over the tea towels.

'*What's* not right?'

'Him.' She jerks her head towards the porch, the front door. 'Going to church.'

Because Gordon lives with Derek; they live together.

'Mum, you're not religious.' The second time today that I have had to remind her.

She places the pile of tea towels emphatically on the table. 'But that doesn't mean that I don't know what's right and what's wrong.' She picks up and flaps one of the tea towels. 'They're *unhealthy*.'

'Well, they look very healthy, to me.' They have permanent suntans. *By nefarious means*, I have heard Mum say, meaning sunbeds.

'They're *unnatural*.'

Looking over the garden, I argue, 'Weeds are natural but you don't like them.'

Behind me, she slaps the tea towel onto the table. 'Will you stop this?'

I turn around and tell her, '*You started this*: I asked you why I couldn't work for them – remember? – and you started all this.'

She clasps her forehead in a display of exasperation. 'I don't want you to go next door. He shouldn't have contact with children.'

'I'm not a child.' I turn off the kettle and splash water over the granules in the bottom of my cup. 'And, anyway, where's *your* licence?'

'I don't need a licence,' she has begun re-folding the tea towel, 'I'm normal.'

'You think so?'

She freezes, dramatically. 'What did you say?'

I make a show of my silence, closing my mouth hard.

'Lola,' she lowers and smooths the square of cloth, the foundation for her new pile of folded tea towels, 'there are young men in and out of that house all the time.'

'So?' I puncture the surface of my drink with a dribble of milk. 'There are young women in and out of this house all the time, but that doesn't mean that we're up to anything with them.'

A glance bounces towards me, and away again.

'And who do you expect them to have in and out of there? Maiden aunts?'

Two tea towels down and several more to go, she gives up and hurries into the hallway. 'I'm late,' she calls back, and, 'get dressed.' And, finally, from the porch, 'I don't care what you say, it's *not normal*.'

*   *   *

Normal: man, woman, children. So, what are *we*? It is three years, now, since Dad told Mum that he wanted a divorce, and moved into somewhere new with Auntie Doreen from three doors down. Three years since our house was sold and the four of us moved here to Corner Cottage. Three years, and Mum still says that we are *New-to-the-neighbourhood*. Last autumn, Gordon and Derek moved into the derelict house next door and began renovations. Why do we know them as Gordon and Derek, when, to them, Mum remains Mrs Judd? Perhaps she has never told them to *Call-me-Angelina*: almost a year, and no *Call-me-Angelina*. Last Christmas, a card came from *Gordon and Derek*, big names, splashes of ink, like autographs; but Mum's reply – small, neat, and carefully joined-up – was *From all at Corner Cottage*.

Three weeks, now, since my holiday began. This morning I lay for a while on the sunlounger with a tea towel draped over my eyes to block the sunlight. Mum was tackling the washing line, flapping pillowcases and swearing at wasps. Suddenly she said, 'Hellooo.' Her voice was directed away from me. I pushed the tea towel back onto my forehead and opened my eyes. Mum was standing on tiptoe, peering over the fence into Gordon and Derek's garden. I knew from the tone of her voice that this exclamation was no mere greeting, I knew better than that: this was an enquiry, *Who-are-YOU?*

The reply came obligingly from the other side of the fence: 'Hiya, I'm Tilly.'

'Hello, Tilly.' She did not move, she wanted more information.

'I'm doing their housework,' her answer came eventually, 'twice a week.'

'Oh, are you?' More information required.

'Yes.' This was said a little unsurely: she was a stranger to Mum's tactics. Vinnie and I would have said, *Well, no, actually, funnily enough, that was a barefaced lie.*

'It's a lovely old house,' said Mum, turning to gaze at it. What was she hoping to see that she had not already seen during all these months of craning over the fence? She has no interest in the house; her interest is in the inhabitants. 'A lovely old house.' Pointedly, no mention of the inhabitants.

'Yes.' The tone remained happy.

There was a pause.

'Well,' said Mum, 'see you again, no doubt.'

'Mondays-and-Fridays,' sang the voice, implying cheerful resignation, unquestionable regularity.

I managed to shift the tea towel back over my eyes before Mum reached me.

'Did you hear *that*?' she breathed over me.

'Could I fail to hear that? Along with everyone else in the neighbourhood.'

A little later, when Mum was indoors, I heard a radio on the other side of the fence. Radio One had never blared before from Gordon and Derek's garden. Mum likes Radio Two; Vinnie and I have to fight hard for Capital. Whenever I hear Radio Two, I am tortured by my visions of the people who sing the jingles: a choir of ex-dancers from *The Andy Williams Show* who wear sky-blue catsuits and have pageboy haircuts? Gordon and Derek's radio tends to murmur voices: usually the urgent but restrained voices of newsreaders, sometimes the hectoring of a quizmaster and the easy smoky banter of the panel, the appreciative laughter of the studio audience welling and retreating over coughs and buzzers. More often during the summer there is the rustle of the cricket commentary. When I heard Radio One, I peeked through a hole in the fence and saw a pair of hands dipping into a full laundry basket. They were bony white hands, ribbed with ink-stain veins. A small round bone rolled in a socket on each wrist. The fingers snapped at a handkerchief in the basket, and I backed away.

Everything that I know about Gordon and Derek's house, I know from the hole in the fence. I have never been inside the house or the garden. But Gordon and Derek have a lot of visitors. Mum often rushes from the washing line to announce, *There are fwendies next door again for dwinkies.* And then we will hear cheerful voices rising and falling, so that the garden sounds like a swimming pool without splashes. They have had drinks for the Amateur Dramatics, a garden party for Italian Intermediate, and a barbecue for the Cricket Club. We were invited on each occasion but Mum always had an excuse.

Now Mum has sent me into our front garden to fetch Georgia's bike. 'What's that doing there?' she shrieked from the lounge, where she is on the phone to Grandma. This shriek will have grated on Grandma, who, last year, told me, *Your mother has let herself go*; who fails to see that it was Dad who did the letting go.

'What? Where?' I replied between mouthfuls of cold tinned rice pudding.

'Georgia's bike!' she screamed. 'What's Georgia's bike doing out there in the front garden?'

I tried, 'Grazing?'

But she was not amused, she screamed louder: 'Go and fetch that bike, please, Lola. *Now*, please, Lola, before some gypsies decide to try their luck.' Then I heard her return her attention to the phone, sighing irritable comments into the mouthpiece: comments about Georgia and me, probably, and then Vinnie, for good measure; and then, probably, her favourite complaint, *Am I made of money? Do these kids of mine think that I'm made of money?*

When I passed the doorway, I told her, 'Fear not, I'll give chase.'

She looked up and narrowed her eyes.

'Mind you,' I added, gliding from her view, 'they'll not get very far. No one gets far on a Ladyshopper.'

Now, stepping into the driveway, I see Tilly on the doorstep of Gordon and Derek's house, smoking. Her eyes are unfocused in the cloud of smoke which is moving stiffly from her slack mouth into the hot still air and clinging to her hair. Her face is angular, regular, unmarked; unlike mine, with dimples, pimples, freckles, mole, snub nose, crooked teeth. Her skin a clear film on the surface of her skull, her pale hair is pulled tightly into a ponytail. How old is she? Older than me, slightly? Suddenly I realize that she reminds me of Mum, of Mum in the old days. Suddenly I realize how much Mum has changed: how gravity has taken a toll on her most delicate parts, made her flesh loose on the underside of her arms, beneath her chin, around her neck, and thickened her hands and ankles, the very places where she should taper. Now Tilly sees me, and smiles by widening her eyes and raising her faint eyebrows. No, not quite a smile but a signal. I try something similar in return as I step back indoors with the bike, the shade of the hallway speckling the inside of my eyelids.

Four weeks since school ended, and today I am writing to my French penfriend, Claudette, in the hope of a free stay sometime in France. *Aujourd'hui il fait chaud, comme d'habitude*. Mum has insisted that I use her old school dictionary, which she fetched for me from the loft. *Zut alors*. Now she interrupts me again, her shadow falling from the doorway onto my paper.

'She's there again,' she slurs excitedly through a mouthful of pegs.

'It's Friday, she comes on Mondays and Fridays, so of course she's there.'

'She's a sweet kid.'

I suspect that she has never seen Tilly smoking on the doorstep. She hates all smokers. She told Vinnie, last week, that if he ever came home again smelling of cigarettes, she would wash him down with carbolic acid. I think she meant soap.

'A very sweet kid,' she says again, stretching, blocking even more sunlight.

Whenever I see Tilly, she gives me the unsmiling smile. It is an acknowledgement rather than a greeting, as if she has been expecting me to be there – at my bedroom window, or on the patio, or behind the fence, or in the shed – and as if she regards us as co-conspirators.

'She always says hello.'

'That's because you say hello *to her*. What do you expect her to do? Ignore you and walk away?'

Sunlight springs back onto the page, and Mum wanders

over to me. 'She always looks cheerful,' her face swoops close to mine, 'which is more than you can manage.'

I slap down my pen.

She moves away, to the window. 'I wouldn't want to work in there,' she peers into the garden, 'because that house lacks a woman's touch.'

That house: through the hole in the fence I have seen a cascade of green velvet curtain at the french windows; from the road I have seen a bowl of roses on the windowsill.

'No kids' mess, though,' I say.

'Well, no,' she concedes, bending to the vegetable rack to choose some bakers from the pile of potatoes.

I have had five weeks of this freedom, now. I can see the postman in the distance, passing from house to house by jumping over borders and rockeries. Next week, he will arrive here with my exam results. I am waiting for Mum; we are going shopping in town before she goes to work.

'Just you wait and see,' Mum shouts from the bathroom. 'Just because we're late, that bus will be early today for the first and only time in its life.'

I step down from the doorstep. Gordon is loading the green van with cardboard boxes. I step back onto the doorstep.

But he has seen me: 'Good morning, Lola!' he shouts over the bushes, with a wave of a tough, tanned hand.

I smile in reply.

'And is life treating you well?'

I shrug.

'Good morning, Mrs Judd, and what a lovely dress, if I may say so.'

Perhaps not her *worst* dress, but I would never have gone so far as to say *lovely*.

Mum pushes past me and peers warily at Gordon. 'Thank you. And good morning.'

'We're off today for two weeks of sun, sea and sand,' he continues, cheerily.

I can sense Mum thinking *Sex*.

'I'm picking Derek up from the office at lunch time, and off we go!'

Mum swings her shopping bag against her shins. 'Going somewhere nice?' She glances up the road towards the bus stop.

'Chianti country,' he bellows, slamming the door of the van.

Mum frowns, puzzled.

To me, *Chianti* sounds Indian.

'Lovely,' Mum shouts to him, as she begins to hurry down the driveway. 'Driving?'

'Oh, no,' he laughs, all tanned twinkles, 'Heathrow.'

'Safe journey, then.' Suddenly she stops, so that I nearly bump into her. 'But what about the cat?'

Gordon and Derek have a tabby, Dolores.

Gordon flaps a chamois leather. 'Oh, our lovely lady, Tilly, has promised to come in twice a day to feed her. In return for holiday pay.' Momentarily, he bites his lip. 'Have you met Tilly?' he asks, but much more quietly. I sense that he feels that he has failed in some obscure rite of neighbourliness by not having introduced her to us.

'Oh, yes,' Mum says, confidently.

'*Love*ly *la*dy,' he confirms, almost sings in praise.

*   *   *

Gordon and Derek had been gone for four days now.

'She's there again,' I tell Mum. The bike is there again; the boy is there again.

Mum says nothing.

On the first day that Gordon and Derek were away, Mum went to the fence when she heard Tilly in the garden in the evening; and from my bedroom, I heard their chatter. A few moments later, Mum breezed past my door with a pile of towels and announced happily, 'She wants to be a nurse.' Like Mum; unlike me. Mum wanted to be a nurse and then she wanted me to be a nurse. I wanted to be a vet and now I want to be nothing.

The day before yesterday, I saw Tilly arrive on the back of a motorbike, or, rather, on the back of the driver, a boy: they were Siamese twins, cupped, bound in jeans and leather jackets. They did not remove their helmets but swung from the bike and snaked behind the hedge towards the house with black bloated heads. The bike was in the driveway for an hour or so.

Yesterday there were three bikes in the driveway for three hours, and the rasp of reggae from the corner of the garden that we cannot see from our house. I watched Mum frowning at the bikes from her bedroom window; she spent three hours in her bedroom with a duster, a can of polish, a feather duster, wet cloths, and the Hoover.

Today there is one bike and no noise. So we are going into our garden. Mum settles on her sunlounger, knitting. I sit on the grass and spread the newspaper beside me. The sole sound is the chirp of the knitting needles. The needles, long thin bones at the end of Mum's fingers, are flashing in the sunshine. They are flashing a code for the pattern. I know nothing about knitting. I sift through the newspaper for the TV page and then scan the schedule for the evening: a mini-serial at nine o'clock, continuing for half an hour after the *News at Ten*. Reading about the mini-serial, I hardly hear the sound from Gordon and Derek's garden, the three sounds; or perhaps I hear them as the signal for the mumble of the newsreader, the hourly high-pitched beeps. But now I hear them again. I stop, pressing the newspaper into the grass, and listen. There are more beeps, four, and I can hear that they are filled with breath, Tilly's breath.

The needles have paused. I glance at Mum but she is frowning into her lap. Is she frowning at the knitting, the sunlight, or the sound from next door's garden? The needles resume, sliding against each other. But Tilly's breaths begin again, longer, louder, a tuneless song. The needles continue ticking, faster. Tilly is reaching for something, or moving something: this is how it sounds, hard work and desperation. But no, because I know what I am hearing: I watch films, I know these sounds. I glance again at Mum, wondering whether we should exchange smiles, but she is staring ferociously at the woollen blotch spreading in her lap. Suddenly Tilly's siren drives into the still hot air of the neighbouring gardens: once, twice, three times, a kind of pain; and a broken, final, fourth call. And now silence except for the tut-tutting of Mum's needles. Mum shifts on the sunlounger, wrenching the canvas, drops the knitting onto the grass with a flourish, and says, 'Shall we have a cup of tea?'

Tilly's white forearms lie along the top of the fence like two basking cats. Her chin rests on a lattice of fingers. Presumably she is standing on something; the laundry basket, perhaps.

She is smiling, watching Mum hose the garden. The jet of water chips at the soil in the flowerbed. I have taken refuge on the patio.

'I'm glad that you're here, next door,' she muses.

Mum turns very slightly towards the fence, the jet of water slipping across the surface of the soil.

'I didn't want this job but I do want the money. And, believe me, it's easy money.'

Still Mum does not speak. The jet of water concentrates on the rhubarb.

'Because it's always immaculate in there.' Tilly nods towards Gordon and Derek's house.

The jet switches to the base of a rose bush.

'They don't need me.' She gazes at the soupy soil beneath the roses. 'It was my mum's idea, she collared Gordon in church, said I needed work.' She watches the jet of water arc above the clematis. 'No one says no to my mum.' She laughs joylessly and detaches herself from the fence.

The hands reappear almost immediately with a packet of cigarettes. She cocks the packet at Mum.

'I don't,' mutters Mum.

Tilly turns and jabs the packet towards me. I sense Mum stiffen. I lower my eyes.

'Lovely house.' The voice is muffled. She is craning with a cigarette towards a lit match. She pauses whilst the tip of the cigarette darkens and disintegrates. Then she removes the cigarette and smoke spills from her mouth into our garden. 'Lovely garden, too, and we had fun yesterday with their washing line.' She laughs, coughs, turns over her hard white wrists to reveal red weals.

Water rattles the base of the fence.

'But of course I hate *them*, I hate men like that.'

Mum drops the hose. It stiffens, swells, twists, hisses water into the grass.

'They're good people,' she seethes, as she walks away.

9

STOOD UP AND THINKING
OF ENGLAND

There they go, the little car bunny-hopping from pothole to pothole, back wheels kicking cartoon-clouds of dust. That tin-box, Tizer-red car that they bought when we arrived here. Down the track towards what they call *el pueblo*, which by now I know means *the village*. They play at Spanish, say the odd word in Spanish, as if that is enough to make this place our home. But I know that their *pueblo* is not quite right: sometimes they try too hard, they sway their way through the word, *poo-ay-blow*; other times, too shallow, slap-happy, *pwebla*. Too English.

So, what shall I do today? The same as I do every day, I suppose; the same as I have done every day for the month since we arrived here. The same as I will do every day until school starts, *Spanish* school, when I am supposed to transform into a Spaniard. There is no one here to stop me from doing whatever I like: the catch is that there is nothing to do. Every day I watch the car bounce away, then I return to the darkness of the villa, the darkness of wooden shutters. This darkness is supposed to be cool; but nothing, nowhere, is cool here. Mum complains that if I woke earlier, I would do more with my days. But no time is early enough, here. I know, because I wake in the early hours, two, three, four o'clock. And when I wake in my wood-dark room I am on my back under my sheet like a corpse and the heat is asleep on top of me, wheezing mosquitoes over me. When I surface again, later, six or seven o'clock, the heat is everywhere, all around my room and on the balcony and the patio, lying in wait for me. By nine, the air is swollen with noise. The sounds of the valley evaporate and hover in a dense, fine rain: the chain-saw barking of chained-up dogs, the thumps of quarrying and construction, the relentless chipping into and building onto these hills. Sometimes there are sounds that I cannot place or explain away: the line of cars moving slowly through the valley and the unbroken scream of their horns, a spooky scream which I took to be some kind of siren, some kind of warning, until Mum and Dad's new friends, the Chryslers, explained that this was a wedding convoy.

This is what I do, every day: I have breakfast, to take up some time; I search the kitchen, trying to find something that will do for breakfast, biscuits, usually – soggy Spanish biscuits which melt in my mouth to cover my teeth with a thick almond paste; I have tea without sickly Spanish milk but with a slice from the lemon that Mum and Dad keep in the fridge for their G & Ts; then I sunbathe for a while, but for no reason because I am not going back home, I have no one to whom I will show my tan. And for hours I look over the hills. There is nothing to see, they never change. But they are here, they are everywhere here, and there is nowhere else to look, except the sky, which is hard on my eyes. These hills have been here for – what? – thousands of years? Millions? Mum read aloud from her guide book that, hundreds of years ago, Moors lived here, hiding from Christians. 'Obviously they didn't know,' she laughed, making one of her better jokes, 'that's Jehovah's Witnesses will find you anywhere.' Thousands of years ago, these hills would have encircled the sea, this valley would have been a bay, but nowadays the sea has shrunk away, ten miles away, and these hills have no purpose, they hold nothing. I can see that they were made by water, they have the look of water, there are ripples in the rock, but nowadays they are deadly dry. From here they have the look of pebbles, spectacularly smooth, but up close they prickle with bushes and shower loose stones. From here I stare up at them and they stare me down. I should know every ripple, every ridge, every ribbon of pink or blue, but there is too much to know, I could look all day, every day; which is, I suppose, exactly what I do.

Throughout the day, I drink cold drinks: I love the fizzy lemon here, which sizzles on the roof of my mouth like real lemon; a proper *lemon*ade rather than the fizzy clear syrup that we had back home. In England. From time to time during the day I have a slow shower – slow not by choice but because of low water pressure – and once or twice I wash my hair, then dry off in the sunshine so that I am blonder, now, than I have ever been; blonder, even, than that blonde baby in the family photos, the baby that was me, once upon a time. Washing away my colour, day by day, I look less and less like a Spaniard. Then, dry, I lie in the sun for a while, before, in the middle of the day, returning to the darkness of the villa, where I try to write letters home to my friends finding I have less and less to tell them. Sometimes I step into the sun for a moment, onto the paving stones for a brief moment to burn the soles of my feet, to feel the burn on the hardest skin that I have.

They will not be gone for long, today. Apparently there are only three villas, today, perhaps three hours of work. I know the routine: sweep, swab, tidy, before tackling the bed linen, swapping clean for dirty. Or *soiled*, as Mum would say; *soiled* seems to be a laundry word, a word for laundry. Today she said, 'If you're so bored, why don't you come with us?' *I'll tell you why: because I don't want to have to deal with other people's soiled laundry, that's why. This was your plan, remember, not mine.* Because this is her job, now: cleaning and tidying other people's villas. (Not our own; not that this *is* our *own*, we rent from the owner, Herr Someone-or-other, who has bought himself a bigger villa, now, somewhere else). Not that Mum would say that this was her job, *cleaning and tidying*: no, she and Dad are *Managing Agents*. This was Dad's invention, he likes titles. Before, he was a *Managing Director*. And, before, we had someone to clean and tidy our house, but she was never called a *Managing Agent*, she was called *The Maid*: Maria, from Columbia. Mum is always telling me how everyone envies us, how everyone wants to leave what she and Dad call *the rat race* and come to live in Spain. Not so very different, in a way, from Maria and her relatives: Maria was always telling us how her relatives envied her because she had come to live in a free and rich country; those were her words, *free and rich*. Mum says that I should be happy, that Spain is a lovely place to live, full of cheap fruit and sunshine. But the fruits that I like are raspberries and blackberries, neither of which grow here. And there is too much sunshine, so much sunshine that we have to cover our windows and live in darkness. If Dad had not lost his business, would we have come here? He says that no one was to blame for what happened to the business. *Recession*. Rat race and recession. Bankruptcy and blame.

So, people pay Mum and Dad to clean for them, to help the flow of holiday-makers. To keep a white river of bed linen flowing through the villas. But they have to be careful, in case they are *denounced*: this is the word for when a Spaniard informs the police that a foreigner is working without a permit. So, to the locals, this housekeeping is simply something that Mum and Dad do to help friends. But to the villa owners, Mum and Dad call this *a nice little family business*. They mean that Dean works with them, repairing shutters, fitting shower curtains, watering gardens. Dean is too old – just – to have to go to school. So he can stay English, burning his nose and his knees, and yelling *'Allo mate* to everyone, even to the Germans. He is old enough to have stayed home on his own, if he had wanted; he could have found a job and a room. But he came to Spain, he tells everyone, to *try his luck*. What does he mean by this? I think that Mum and Dad think, hope, that he means work. But I think that he means girls. I overheard him telling one of his friends, before we came here, that Spanish girls are gorgeous. But what would they want with *him*? Not that Mum and Dad would agree: I am surprised that this Spanish sunshine is so important to them because, in their opinion, the sun shines from Dean's every orifice. Mum says that he is good with his hands, which is lucky because he is no good with anything else, like his brain. Certainly he was never any good for the one task required of an older brother: bringing friends home. There was something wrong with each one of the friends of his who hung around our house: horrid long hair; beard; bad breath; too many drugs; pet python.

Sally goes to the villas with them, but to play rather than to work. Because she is ten. Sometimes Mum complains to me, 'Why don't you spend more time with Sally?' *Because she is ten, that's why. Because she plays. I do not play; I am fifteen.* She plays the play of a ten-year-old: she hauls one of those long-necked loungers away from the herd over the crazy paving patio into a patch of shade, then lies flat on her back on its segmented pink-floral-print cushion and whispers up into the sky, makes up stories. Mum and Dad never tell Sally to listen to the tapes, the Spanish lessons, because, they say, she is young, and will *pick things up*. Like bubonic plague, with any luck. No, too cruel, but I do wish that she would stop whispering in her sleep. Whispering, sighing, laughing wearily but politely into the blackness of our small, hot bedroom.

I am supposed to spend my days listening to tapes. The tapes are supposed to help me when I go to school. But I have listened to the tapes a few times and I know that they will not help me.

I would like two tickets to Madrid, please.

Single or return?

A one-way ticket to Madrid, please. But no, because what would I do in Madrid? I want to go to London, not to Madrid. *Londra*.

Can you please direct me to the police station?

Are they joking?

How do you celebrate New Year in your country?

Your country. But this is *my* country, now. Or so Mum and Dad tell me.

Mum and Dad say that I will make friends, in time, here. As soon as I *learn the lingo*, they say. They know that I will have no English friends: the English here are old, retired, their conversations concern the local restaurants, whether *vino y postre* is *inclusivo* on the *menu del dia*; wine and pudding make their days, here. But how will I ever make friends, when I start school, by being able to ask for directions to the police station? The other day I had a massive row with Mum, I wanted to know what would happen to me, here. *Stuck here*, were my words, words which she said were *unhelpful*. She said, 'You're not *stuck anywhere*, Gillian.' Her opinion was that I would do everything that I would have done in England, but in Spain. She said, 'You'll meet a boy, and he'll happen to be Spanish; and you'll marry him, and you'll have children, and they'll be Spanish, and is that so very awful?' For some years I have had an ambition to be Prime Minister; but how can I be Prime Minister of a country where I do not live?

I could escape, but to where? To the *pueblo*? Too far, too hot, even for the pueblo's pool, before sundown. This weather keeps me home. When I do decide to walk to the pool, Mum always calls behind me from the balcony, 'Don't drown, okay?' I hate the walk because I have to pass the dogs: five of them, a family, in a small wire enclosure all day every day with only the shade of a solitary scratchy tree. I have no idea why they are there. In the beginning, from the road, from the car, this was all that I could see, which was bad enough, reminding me of those shoebox-sized cages of canaries lodged in the doorways and windows of houses in the pueblo, those window boxes of birdsong. But then, when I walked alone to the pool, I went down the track to say hello to them. And that was when I saw their bones, the claws of ribs, the Belsen pelvises. They were yelling for me, their noses in the wire and their tails very tall, curved, flagging me down. But what could I do, what can I do? Nowadays I can hardly face them, those shivery noses, those shaky tails. I have no money to buy food for them and there are never enough scraps for five. I want someone to tell me what to do. But I suspect that there is nothing that I can do that will make a difference to them. I have asked the Chryslers but they say that there is no RSPCA and *if you can't stand the sight of a few starving dogs, you'll never survive in this country*. I do not want to survive in this country.

When I reach the pueblo I try to hurry through the sharp, dark gazes of the old men who hunch and scowl under the small black discs of their berets and over the bigger white discs of the tabletops outside the bar in the square. I think that I know how they would prefer me to dress, but I will not wear widows' weeds for anyone. Sometimes, in the evenings, we drive to other towns where the bars feel friendlier and we can watch telly. Often I recognize the pro-gramme, the people in the programme, but they have fake voices. Once, we saw *Dallas*: JR's Texan twang had been scrubbed from the soundtrack and he spoke in a Spanish growl which made me think of a matador even though I have never heard a matador speak. This was like a dream: in dreams, I know who someone is even if she or he has someone else's voice or face; in dreams, this mix of bodies, faces, voices is unimportant, this mix of worlds.

On the edge of the pueblo there is a disco: *Discoteca*, in neon. A whitewashed breeze block cube surrounded by a car park. Whenever I step onto my balcony into near-silence in the early hours, I can hear the pulse and even see the sign far below in the black valley; not the word, *Discoteca*, but a small blur of blue. I want to know if Dean has been there, but he refuses to tell me where he has been when he has borrowed the car. Usually, though, he stays home in the evenings: he comes home late, weary, mucky from having watered lots of gardens; he showers for hours, then eats his way through the kitchen, then lounges over every piece of furniture in turn with his feet up on every other piece, but suddenly he is in his bedroom, drawn into the darkened darkness of his bedroom and sleeping a shuttered sleep.

The end of the day is my favourite time, *my* time, a few hours that no one else seems to know, a few hours that seem to pass everyone by because they are in kitchens, bathrooms, cars, bars, preparing for the coming evening. There is an hour or two when the sun is below the horizon but dusk has not yet inked the sky. And then, for a while, the heat is neither the slashing heat of the day nor the thick heat of the night. And I kid myself that this is no heat at all, that the colourless glaze over the valley is thin, cool air. If I am not at the pool, with nothing on my mind but the number of lengths that I have swum, then I have another favourite place for this favourite time of mine: I like to sit with my back against the back wall of the villa, my barely bikini-strapped back on the white-hot wall in the place where the villa stops and the terraces start; the place from where the terraces start to step away. I am high up, way above the pueblo, looking down on toy cars sliding to and from the main plaza in radial streets; but I am below the villa, the crockery-clattery villa. I am almost hidden and quite alone.

Later, much later, I like to lie on a towel on the balcony in the shiny black sky and search the airwaves for John Peel, edging back and forwards on the illuminated dial through fuzzy French and Spanish and listening for his familiar voice, oddly both doleful and cheerful. And for several hours I track the arc of the blazing moon over me as his voice lisps and fades. The sky, here, is freckled with bluish stars; some of them shiver. So many stars that somewhere, on some of them, there is bound to be life; but because there are so many, we can never know. One less yes-or-no for me to worry over. These times – earlier, my shoulder blades warm on the wall, later, my eyes on the clotted-cream moon – are the only times when I am happy that I have nothing to do, and these times come only when the sun has dropped away.

Recently the days have seemed even hotter than usual because of the fires. This week, I have seen two fires: a week ago, the clean blue skyline showed a smudge of smoke which, later, in darkness, became a weal; and then three days ago, on a hillside near here, the stumpy trees glistened red and the sun was fogged by smoke for hours. So much smoke from nothing much, from scrub and a few sparse olive groves. For a few days a silky layer of ash appeared and reappeared on every exposed surface: the car, the balcony, the patio table and chairs. We wiped and wiped but our cloths turned the ash to mud. Whenever I stood under the spluttery shower, I watched the remains of the smoke sink between my toes and snake along the bottom of the bath to the plughole.

We have heard of people having to leave their homes, speeding away with a car-load of possessions; we have read in the local paper of walkers hurrying down from the hills to the caves but then dying in them from the smoke. A fire can happen anywhere, to anyone. A splinter of glass is enough, the sparkle turning into a spark. So now I spend my days watching helicopters and planes watching the hills for sparks and suspiciously dim hazes. And when they fade into the dusk, I watch alone. As the sky darkens, hardens, I look over the lumpy blackness for red. When we had our fire, I tracked a blue spark over the reddening hill: the beacon of a solitary police car crawling as far as possible into the scrub, as near as possible to the flames. I knew that the police were keeping watch and wondering what to do. But there is never much that they can do. Except warn us. And I do not trust them even to do this, to notice that we are here, or to care that we are here. So when those speedy electric-blue wings of air dropped down and the car slunk back into the pueblo, I stayed on the balcony for a while and then went back three or four times in the early hours to check that we were safe. I saw black trees in the blackness, they lit up as they died.

Sometimes during the day the helicopters and planes drop water from the air, they snap open their trap doors to bomb the flames and I see the waterfalls fizz to vapour. The Chryslers say that one of them, somewhere, sometime, flew too low and was snatched down by flames. Why is there no invention, something clever, something other than water, a foam to cover these tinderbox hills from the rays? Apparently the water comes from swimming pools; the helicopters swoop, hover and suck from the squeaky-clean pools of the holiday-makers. They can choose whichever pool they like, take however much they need: one minute, a mirror full of sky; the next, an empty basin of blue tiles. They do not seem to have touched the pueblo's pool, where, yesterday, the sunken ash stirred and whirled up around me.

Mum and Dad came back from their three villas with a letter for me. Our letter box is in a wall of boxes in the pueblo, a small silver door opened by a tiny key which shivers like a charm on Dad's clanky key-ring. The letter had come by air, flying banners of stamps and *Par Avion* stickers. Sometimes I have letters from friends but this was a note from Tracy King who is not quite a friend but was in my class. She is coming to Spain with her family on holiday next week, to a town which is slightly less than an hour's drive from here. *Do drop over*, she writes, *for lazy days and crazy nights!*

She has written on airmail paper, turquoise and noisy, in primary school handwriting, the letters formed and joined exactly how she was told to form and join them all those years ago. Tracy King is neither *lazy* nor *crazy*, and nor, I suspect, are her days and nights, even on holiday. She is famous for her mother; her mother is famous because she is on the PTA Committee, and every other committee, most of which are her own inventions. Her mother fund-raises, organizes, supervises. She wears make-up that looks like make-up, she constructs her face from foundation and blusher and her teeth look false. Tracy takes after her down to the double chin and fiercely folded arms, and her eyelashes look like weapons. She is bustly, busty, fussy, fond of pleats; she is bossy although no one takes any notice. There is a little sister, and I remember that her Dad is rumoured to be having an affair simply because he is so much nicer than her Mum.

The surface of the pool wobbles, threads of sunshine coiling and bouncing like bedsprings. Mr King reaches for his towel, water sliding from him and steaming on the paving stones. He is so brown, so smoothly and uniformly brown, that from here his skin looks like fur, or velvet. Tracy, her mum and her sister Karen have to be careful: they are striped with sunburn and strap marks, they have burned in strips and slabs in colours ranging from uncooked dough to tinned meat. Blotchy and pinched by bikinis, they sit in cones of shade, stuck to loungers, the backs of which have been raised like those of hospital beds to prop them up. We are around their pool, their own pool. I am lying on my tummy on my lounger, topping up the tan on my back, feeling the sunshine press on my shoulder blades and pool in the small of my back. I never burn, and, anyway, I am practised, I know exactly what I am doing; and there are very few marks on me because we live so far from anywhere that there are plenty of private places where I can undo my straps. Around their tummies they each have a roll of flesh, protective and quaint like a rubber ring. I have a very different type of body: the bodies in my family are cradles of bones, we are ribcages and pelvises linked loosely by spines and we can see the precise articulation of each joint in each limb.

Around and underneath their loungers is everything that they need: squeezy bottles of lotion, chilled bottles of chocolate milk, floppy piles of magazines. They drink their dense, dark milk through curly, joke straws. Mum would never buy chocolate milk because of the expense and the calories. But here they seem to survive on it, with chicken and chips. I had chicken and chips with them last night; I was staying for the night and we went out for a meal, the choice of restaurant having been put to a vote. In the restaurant, I was trying to be brave, probing beneath the crackling skin to strip the feeble bones, trying to cope with the slimy pink-streaked flesh which made me think of blood-stained phlegm, when Mrs King came to the rescue with a snowy forkful from her own plate. 'There,' she murmured, tapping another forkful on to my plate, then another. Now, from her lounger, she is calling to her husband, 'Gilly needs a top up, Dickie.' I know that she means another bottle of the milk, this is the term that she likes to use, to drawl: *a top up*.

I raise my head, look up into a bank of chlorine-spiked sunshine. 'I'm fine, thanks.'

'Relax,' she tells me.

I *am* relaxed. 'Really,' I try again, 'I'm fine.' In fact I am *full*.

'Dickie,' she says conclusively.

'Absolutely,' he confirms. I can hear that he is circling the pool, his bare soles clicking on the paving stones, the spilled water lisping. He is breathing roughly, he was only in the pool for a moment or two, having dived in to cool off. Whereas we like to shuffle reluctantly into the deepening and freezing water up to the tops of our thighs, the point when suddenly there is no going back; and then, with screams, we throw ourselves forward. My head smashes down, the surface becomes a thin silvery-blue line over my brow, the water roars into my ears and my breath becomes noisy. Then, half-acclimatized already, we spend quite a while lolling in the water, or clinging to the walls, our drenched hair drying into ringlets.

'You're on holiday,' Tracy's mum purrs to me, 'enjoy yourself.' I have already been invited back for the last two nights of their holiday.

'Girls,' *her* girls, now, 'are you okay?' *For chocolate milk*.

'Top up, please.'

'Me too, Daddy.'

'And a little *vino tinto* for me, Dickie, darling.'

She is so keen for them to enjoy themselves. If my mum asks us if we are okay, her question is more like an accusation. Usually she simply warns us, *Don't drink all of that at once*.

Mr King bends to pick up a bottle of suntan lotion from beneath Tracy's lounger. 'Petal,' he says to Karen, 'have you bathed in any asses' milk, recently?'

'*Daddy*,' she giggles.

'Well,' he lobs the bottle gently and accurately onto the end of her lounger, 'I don't want my fair-skinned princess to turn into a blister.'

Tracy's mum speaks to me: 'You look super with your hair so much blonder, you know.'

I smile; yes, I do know.

'Whoever would have thought that there was a blonde bombshell hidden away in that brunette!'

But *I* knew; and there were others who seemed to know, too. And, anyway, I was never a brunette; she must have been trying to avoid saying *mouse*. Her own hair is mousy, with highlights which are anything but; they have turned her grey. Tracy has a perm, a style which comes close to corkscrew curls.

'Have you seen Lucinda Lightfoot's mother, lately?' Tracy's mum asks all of us, asks no one in particular, 'Have you *seen* that perm?'

No one replies: no, no one seems to have seen Luce Lightfoot's mum since she had a bob; but our imaginations are beginning to whir.

'Not that perm is the word, really. Complete and utter mistake is the word.'

Gossip, again, but in her laid-back style: unlike my mum, who questions, probes, then turns sniffy and disapproves *of us*. Tracy's mum lives in our world, in an odd way: from her committees, she knows people who we know. Sometimes she has insider information for us.

Karen pipes, 'Mrs Lightfoot? *Her?* More like Mrs Heavy-boots.'

Her mum laughs, 'Oh, Sweetie.'

Mr and Mrs King laugh *with* Tracy and Karen; my mum and dad laugh *at* Dean, Sally, and me.

But now Mrs King turns serious: 'Unlucky woman, that daughter of hers hanging around with that drug-taking crowd.'

Clubbing crowd. This is not insider information, this is something that everyone knows.

Tracy pipes, 'Luce could be very pretty if she tried.'

'Yes,' a note of surprise from her mum, 'yes, I suppose so.'

If she *tried*? A trying prettiness, like Tracy's prettiness: like a newly-upholstered chair, expensive, solid, and scratchily sparkly. Luce *is* pretty, but her prettiness is a different kind. A real kind. I remember that she has brown hair and an olive tone to her skin which is similar to the foundation which Tracy wears when she is going somewhere special. But Luce's colour could never come from make-up. Tracy's foundation tends to look thick and dark yellow like damp sand. But now she is wearing nothing but a bikini and the polish which is hardening on her toenails. She has cotton wool like bunnies' bobtails between her candied toes. Like this, she is prettier than I have ever seen her. Unarmed of her shoulder-bag, round-shouldered in her bikini, she is prettily puppy-fatted. But this evening she will squeeze into a dress and sharpen her features with eye- and lip-pencils for our trip to her local disco.

My bed is a haven from the daytime hardness of sunshine and cold water. This sheet, tucked to tighten slightly over my legs, to bind me to the bed, has closed around my feet like cupped hands.

Only now do I realize that there has been no word from Tracy for a while. I listen for her, and tune into the buzz and hum of deepening sleep. And I warm to her: hard-nosed Tracy become slack; square-shouldered Tracy rolled into crooks and folds. I know that even in my sleep I have been thinking about coming back here, looking forward to coming back here. I have been lying here but my thoughts have been thinking themselves, they have been running even when I have been turned from them. Since I came to this country, this is the only kind of sleep that I have had: every morning I wake bemused, aware that I have been kept busy. The less I do during the day, the busier I am in my sleep. What was Tracy saying, before she fell asleep? Her words had become slower, her voice had seemed to come from somewhere smaller than usual, which had made her sound sad.

She has had no gossip for me, I have realized that she has no news because there has been no school for a month: her life, like mine, has been stopped for the summer months, the detail in our lives has been bleached by the sun. Before she fell asleep, she asked about Pedro. And she mentioned Rory: her only mention of him, in two days. And a shy mention. And I had always thought of her as fearlessly nosy. Fearsomely nosy. For two days I had known that I owed him something more than this silence; I knew that if I could mention him, I would be not simply speaking *of* him but somehow speaking *up* for him. But how could I introduce him into the conversation? *Remember Rory?* And then what? What if she simply said yes? What would I say? *Well, so do I.* Well, of course I do.

Since we moved here, I have been taking change coin by coin from Mum's purse, day by day, and banking this booty in a sock in my drawer. And every week or so, on an evening when I am walking home alone from the pool, I detour into the phone box and use this small sum to call Rory, who tries to call me back. But lately we seem to have had nothing much to say to each other. And this nothing much is quite unlike the nothing much which made our phone calls so long when I lived down the road from him. Nowadays our hurried, coin-devouring conversations allow no time to do anything other than swap news. And this summer there has only been so much news to swap. Whenever I am standing there inside the steel frame of the pueblo phone box, listening to the fizzle of the invisible line between us, I remember how we would lie together for hours on the settee or in the park. I remember how I loved the warmth of him. But there is so much warmth here: how would we have been if we had grown up here? What I loved was to have him close to me. But now he is a thousand miles away.

Earlier, this black hush was jangling with Tracy's tapes, and shimmering with clothes, jewellery, and powder puffed from the clamping jaws of our compacts. The scorch of deodorant in the air was enough to shrivel the mosquitoes. With my mascara wand, I turned my eyelashes into wings; my opened, darkened eyes watched my face emerge as if from sleep. Little Karen was perched on Tracy's bed, her bare thighs the shape and colour of milk bottles. 'Here,' she would command Tracy, and then fasten a button or straighten a skewed seam. Her running commentary seemed to be made from someone else's lines, she sounded like a child in an American sitcom: 'Breathe in and think of England.' Sometimes she and Tracy did a double act: 'Mummy met Daddy at a dance, but at first she thought that he was a spiv . . .'

So that Tracy fed her the next line, 'But *then* . . .'

'Well, *then* . . .' and then I heard how their mum had been won over.

From time to time, their mum's face loomed around the door, extending her ribbed neck before popping back into the darkness to make a show of leaving us to ourselves. She made a show of envying us, too; she wanted us to enjoy ourselves and she wanted us to know that we were enjoying ourselves: 'I wish that I was going with you,' then, later, 'Think of me, girls, stuck home with a grumpy old Hector.'

To which Karen objected, 'Poor Daddy!'

Her mum bared her teeth in an impression of a smile. 'Oh, don't you worry about poor old Daddy, he's lucky to have me.'

She wants Tracy to have a boyfriend. As far as I know, Tracy has never been involved with anyone. But during my two days here her mum has hardly stopped mentioning Peter Lawley. Peter Lawley was two years above us, and next year he is Head Boy. These name-drops seem to imply that he has something to do with Tracy, but he seems to have more to do with her mum. Karen copies, telling little stories which have no point other than that they revolve around him. And then their dad remembers to fall into line, with an occasional playful hitch of an eyebrow, 'Oh, *Peter* . . .' Tracy smiles but says nothing; Peter Lawley seems to be a friend of the family rather than her own.

We did not want to leave for the disco before half-past ten. Tracy's mum agreed, explaining to her husband that, 'This is the continent, nothing gets going until late.'

He laughed, 'Except the mosquitoes, because I'm eaten alive every evening at dinner.'

Karen piped, 'Can I stay up and drive there with them?'

The late start allowed us to negotiate to be fetched after midnight, at half past. Tracy's dad decided, 'Seems reasonable.' And her mum smiled, drawled, 'My little pumpkins.'

Later, when we drove away, the tyres growling in the gravel, she called from the patio, 'Be good, and if you can't be good, be careful.'

Tracy hooted a laugh.

When we arrived, Tracy's dad gave us extra money in case we should need a taxi in an emergency, and found us a nearby rank. Outside the disco, we strained to hear his instructions over the careless slams of car doors and the thumps of the music through the walls. Everyone seemed to know one another, they crowded around their cars, *on* their cars, tipping beer bottles to raised, parted, fish-like lips.

'Remember,' Mr King's face delved for seriousness, 'two drinks, no more.'

Tracy tittered, 'Doubles.'

Inside, the dance floor was hardly larger than the spherical mosaic of mirror which rotated overhead. The bass beat knocked through my ribs and motorized my heart. I followed Tracy to the bar, where we bought our drinks. The rum smelled like glue in the Coke. All around us, perfumes and aftershaves cloaked their wearers like masks. We stood in front of a mural of a palm tree which was symmetrical and pert, quite unlike the real, reptilian, prehistoric growths of scales and spikes in the car park. I was standing there, by the mural, when I saw Pedro. I saw him and in a minute or two my soul was drawn to him like the measured, mysterious draining of my shower-water back down to the earth and towards the equator. I knew what I was here to do, I knew that I could still do this. He was lolling on the bar with a friend and in a sense there was nothing particularly striking about him: he was tall, slim, nice-looking, in jeans. But his teeth and the whites of his dark eyes and the shine on his black hair seemed to me to burn like the brilliance that people claim to see beyond the darkness when they are dying, the brilliance that draws them forward.

I turned to Tracy. 'Time for my second drink, I think.'

Her eyes widened, her blank gaze dropped to my full glass. 'Trust me,' I said.

And that was how I ended up next to Pedro, which is why he turned to me, and when we spoke. And this was all that we did, for the whole evening: somehow we talked, easily, for hours, even though my Spanish is limited to shopping and his English to textbook introductions. I was careful not to betray Tracy's trust: I talked to her, too, I never stopped talking to her; I talked *for* her to Pedro's friend because they were obviously keen on each other. Not quite keen enough, in her case, in the end, because eventually she saw some people whom she knew from the beach, went over to say hello, stayed with them and became heavily involved in a conga. Pedro and I had to lean close to each other to catch the words which travelled like whispers but had been spoken loudly. I watched his mouth work on unfamiliar words: his face worked hard, and he smiled harder.

The time was taken by this slow turning of words, and only now do I realize that I had had no idea of what to do, what was expected of me or what could or should happen or not happen between us; only now do I realize that in a foreign country, even this, especially this, is a foreign language. But why did I lie, why did I leave untouched his unspoken assumption that I live in England? When he asked if I would come to the disco again, I told the truth: Thursday.

When we had to leave, Tracy squeezed my shoulder and

reassured me, 'I'll tell Dad that you're on your way,' then turned to Pedro to chime, 'Ciao,' before ambling away over the car park, her stiletto heels croaking on the concrete. And this was when Pedro and I had our kiss, this was when the small space that had been between us was turned inside out. A mere minute or two of kissing but I was shaking, so much so that I could have been a cartoon character who cracks and crumbles into pieces. By the time that we stepped back from each other, I had forgotten how to say goodnight in any other way, and could only smile as I turned away.

Tracy leaves tomorrow. I am supposed to be there with her, now, but I am trapped here. By rain. *The rain in Spain*, Sally chirps whenever she moves to a window. She leaves this *rain in Spain* in the air because there is no more to say; no hope for us of any plane. Or car, because the road to the pueblo is flooded, the dip in the road has become a deep pond. This morning, in one of the lulls in the storm, Dad drove down very slowly with Dean, their tyre-tracks two deep sluices. When they returned ten minutes later, the vivid mud had turned our car tabby-coloured.

Slamming his streaked and speckled door, Dad shouted up to the balcony, 'No go: too much water in the dip.' This was news to us, this had been the only trip down the road in two days.

Sally squealed, 'Will we starve, then? Or will they drop supplies for us?'

Sprinting up the steps, Dean mumbled to Mum, 'If you're desperate, I can wade through.'

'Action Man,' I said.

'Fat chance of starvation,' Mum told us. 'We need to finish

up the contents of the freezer box.' Because there has been no electricity for two days.

Nor water: every turn of a tap brings a parched strain, but no water. When Mum discovered that we had no water, she remembered, 'The Chryslers told me that this would happen: when there's no power, the local pump packs up.'

So, Sally's other little joke is, *Water, water, everywhere* . . .

There is enough to drink, in bottles; but what I want is a bath: all I want, now, is a bath. I want warmth; I want the hard white shine of the bathroom; I want to lock a door on my family.

For two days we have been here in the main room, surrounded by candles stuck onto saucers and towels rucked beneath doors and heaped into the fireplace to soak up leaks. The towels swell and smell. Because there is no electricity, we have no music to drown the roar of rain on the roof. Mum has returned to her roots, to the olden days, writing letters all the time: bowing over her pen and paper in a halo of candlelight, she looks like a Victorian lady. She is even wearing glasses, the reading glasses that she never normally wears because she never normally reads or writes. The next time that she criticizes me, I can say *Boys don't make passes* . . .

Our candles are a shiny, slimy white; they are, in Dad's cross words to Mum, *a false economy*: each one pools on the saucer within a couple of hours and then we are one snuffed wick closer to darkness. Whenever anyone has to go to the bathroom, we are one candle down and darker.

When we try to sleep, we are woken by a swell of the storm. Last night I was woken by the sound of someone falling down as a dead weight on to the floor upstairs; but in a moment I remembered that there is no upstairs here: I realized that this was thunder, again. Sally ran to Mum and Dad's bedroom, and stayed with them. For an hour or so I lay listening to the storm, the rips in the sky above me. The chinks in my shutters were pale and pulsing, the sky was never free from lightning. Today I am so tired, the darkness that I see around my eyes in the mirror is more than shadow thrown by the candle. All that I want now is to melt into a tub of clean, steaming water; I want to close my strained eyes and stop time, stop the painfully slow turn of time, I want to surface only when everything is back to normal. I cannot quite believe that everything will not be normal when I next look; but somehow, at the same time, I have forgotten how the world was ever any different from this, any better than this.

Yesterday I went to the windows or onto the covered balcony every quarter of an hour or so to check for any break in or lightening of the cloud. From the windows I could see nothing but pus-yellow smoke, a kind of cloud that I had never seen before. On the balcony, I was stunned by the sizzle of the rain in the mud where our road had been. Mum kept telling me to be patient. She said that the Chryslers had told her that this weather would come, that the summer would break like this, with storms and rain for a couple of days. She told me, 'Your problem is that you haven't learned to take the rough with the smooth.' She is always so keen to tell me about the problems she thinks that I have. She seems to think that I have a lot of them. 'This weather is only for a couple of days,' she said. 'Once a year for a couple of days.'

But not *this* couple of days, surely: why *this* couple of days, *my* couple of days?

'Tracy will understand,' she decided, earlier today. 'She'll know what has happened, she knows that you're stuck up in the hills.'

You said it. I was stuck up in the hills, staring into the silvery veil of rain, when I should have been having a laugh with the Kings. And I knew that, in a few hours' time, thirty miles down the coast, Pedro would assume that he had been stood up. He would give up on me and I would never find him again. Earlier, on several occasions when the rain ebbed for a while, I tried to persuade Dad, and even Dean, to take me, to take a chance, to take the risk, but eventually Dad decreed that, rain or no rain, the roads are dangerous and no one is going anywhere.

Staying by the window, I remembered the dogs, the family of starved dogs in their enclosure on bare ground, beneath the feeble tree. Would they survive? *How could* they survive? But how would they die; do – how do – animals die of rain? What did they feel, what would they make of this sudden, total change in their world? When I came away from the window, trying to stop thinking, Dad and Dean had gone to the garage to service the car. *Making good use of their time*, as Mum wasted no time in telling me. The car that should have been taking me to freedom was being taken to pieces. For other, future trips, trips in a future that seemed to have nothing to do with me. Cleaning the engine with filthy cloths, Dad and Dean would need our precious water to wash their hands: *Making bad use of our water*, I replied to Mum.

A little later, on the balcony, I could hear them: those intermittent wordless utterances of satisfaction or concern, the indecipherable language of men who are working on something mechanical. Back indoors, Sally had begun to organize games, formal games for which she had to find boards and packs of cards in cupboards and drawers. Now she has played for hours with everyone but me.

Mum keeps telling me to *come away from that window*. Once she added, 'This is no one's fault, you know, Gillian.'

This is your fault, for going bankrupt, for coming here, for making me come here with you.

In twenty-four hours' time, Tracy will have flown through this rain; she will be home, watching *Only Fools and Horses* or something.

Earlier Mum had said, 'You can write to her.' And now she keeps telling me that *This is not the end of the world*.

How little she knows.

10

DON'T TOUCH IT, DON'T IGNORE IT, STAY CALM

Earlier today, I was called to my daughter's school because she had said fuck to the headmaster. Not that this was what I was told, of course: I was told, by his secretary, that there had been some trouble. She called me, on his orders, to ask me to fetch Sylvie: *I'm afraid that there has been some trouble, involving your daughter. Could you please come and fetch her?* What she did not tell me was that Sylvie was refusing to leave. Perhaps I should have known: trouble is nothing new, but I had never been called to *fetch* her. I rushed to the school. As I ran down the corridor towards the office, towards the headmaster who stood in his open doorway, I called, 'I'm dreadfully sorry,' and then I heard her, *'Don't fucking apologize for me.'*

I went into the office, saying, 'Enough.'

She was occupying a chair on the nearside of the desk, one of the two chairs which are for parents. Her mouth resembled a piece of wire, thin but tough; her chin was cocked; her arms were folded too high for comfort. But her shoes did not quite reach the ground. She told me, 'No, it is *not* enough, *nothing* is enough for these people,' and announced, 'I'm staging a sit-in to protest against vivisection in the biology labs,' started to explain, 'they *butcher animals . . .*'

I murmured, 'I'll butcher *you*,' before turning to the head-master, 'I'm so sorry, Mr Gray, but she has been working rather hard, lately.'

He stepped – *swaggered* – into the room. 'Unfortunately, I have seen no evidence of that, Mrs Rees. And your daughter has informed me that she fails to give an expletive deleted for scientific progress.'

'Not at the *expense of lives*,' she corrected, before appealing to me, 'you don't know what they *do* . . .'

I told him, 'My name is not Mrs Rees; Rees was my married name.' I was sure that I saw a smirk. 'Is that funny?' I turned and pointed to Sylvie, '*You*,' then pointed to the door, '*out*.'

She slid forward in the chair, to implore, '*Mum* . . .'

I stood my ground, did not lower my arm.

So she slipped from the chair, strode to the doorway and away. I heard the secretary, in the corridor, adding her dis-approval: '*Well*.'

In this confusion, I turned to the headmaster and said, by mistake, 'I'll talk to *you later*.'

Sylvie hurried ahead to the bus stop, pausing only to whirl around and scream, '*So, you think that they should be allowed to cut up mice and frogs*.'

She was so far ahead of me that I had to shout: '*I think that there are other ways to win hearts and minds*.'

And then there were no more words between us: we stood in silence in the bus shelter. I was thinking my way through the crisis, deciding to ring the headmaster when we reached home, to apologize and try to gauge the depth of Sylvie's disgrace. To discover if she would be allowed back into school, and if so, when. The corner of my eye vibrated with her pacing, craning, tapping, frowning, her show of im-patience and contempt. Turning away, weary, I wondered: did she act alone, or were there others, who gave up, gave in and left her there? I knew that it was quite likely that she had acted alone: she is an accomplished lone operator. Perhaps because she is an only child. So I did not waste my breath, risk disappointment by demanding, *Who put you up to this?*

The bus came, and I followed her up the steps but was left to pay for her. Which was fair enough, I suppose: she had not asked to be taken home. When I turned around, I saw that she had gone towards the back, to one of the two long seats that are turned from the others to face into the aisle. I went to the opposite one, because it would have seemed odd to perch next to her, so close yet unable to see her. But then we travelled for ten minutes without exchanging a glance. Ten unbroken minutes. Her eyes avoided mine. I do not think that I have gazed at her for so long since she was a baby.

She was slumped, her shoulders slipped sideways but the soles of her shoes still not quite low enough to reach the footplate. She did not look unhappy: and of course not, because she was away from school, on her way home, with time to think up new plans. Suddenly I wondered: what do other people see, when they looked at her? Not those who know her, not my friends or her teachers, but the people on the bus: what did they see? A pretty, petite sixteen-year-old. Even if *petite* is no longer a word with much currency away from dress shops, and *pretty* no longer a compliment, I believe, to which girls particularly aspire. I imagine that Sylvie would prefer *sultry*, or something. Which is tough, because she is pretty, just plain pretty: despite dabbling with lipstick and mascara, she has a natural look, one which reminds me of sun-warmed wood. She is very unlike me: I am a natural *and* bottle blonde. I like to keep on the bright side of blonde;

and I know that grey is supposed to make the victim look distinguished, but I am a dumpling and nothing would make me look distinguished, not even if I took to wearing a monocle.

Presumably in other people's eyes, the eyes of people on buses, Sylvie is a dream daughter. But they do not know about her conscience, and how her conscience has very little to do with dreams. She lives to the tick of her conscience, utterly without compromise. She has never turned her combative gaze from anyone. Apart from me, even though there have been only the two of us since she was three years old. But I have been careful never to give her much cause for complaint. And I do not count, because there are far more important battles to be won; her campaigns are focused, and focused outwards. She bypasses me, her attention slides in my direction, comes close, and there is a sticky moment, but then she is off on the trail of untruth and hypocrisy.

The problems began in her first week at school – ten years ago – with her plimsolls; where to wear them or where not to wear them, I do not remember the details. Most recently, she decided to boycott her school's compulsory Christianity: when forced to attend assemblies, she whistled through the prayers. Which was when I was called to school to *Discuss the situation*. Which meant, *defuse* the situation. Which I managed, but this time I doubt my chances: a whistle is one problem, an expletive quite another.

We are home, now, but still wordless. I have made some tea, and properly: sloshing the pot with hot water, stirring the leaves. So now we are waiting for the tea to brew. Our silence passes with the silent tick of the leaves around the pot and their turning over into the bottom. I am busying myself with the shopping that I bought earlier, before I was called to the school. I have bought a jumper. The plastic wrapper bears the advice, *To avoid suffocation, keep away from children.* How very true: this shopping seems to come from another world, when the day was simply one of my two half-days off per week, when the day was *my* day, and not yet taken over by Sylvie and reduced to chaos. She is leaning emphatically onto her elbows, onto the table, looking down onto the tabletop.

I have to do this, it is my job as a mother: I open with, 'Do you have to be so *confrontational*?' *Confrontational* was the word used by her headmaster during the row about the whistled prayers.

Her eyes snap up to mine, '*What?*' The tone closer to fury than to irritation.

Don't act dumb, 'You *know* what.'

She drops back in her chair. 'Of course I have-to-be-*so*-confrontational,' the latter words mimicked, but ridiculously, her head wobbly and her eyes wide. 'Confrontation is what this is *about.* These people *need* confronting. The *problem* is that they are *never* confronted with what they are doing, with what they have done.'

I try to suggest, 'Darling, all that you're confronting them with is *you.*'

Her eyes flick to the jumper, 'Do you *need* another jumper?'

'No, I don't *need . . .*' but this is ridiculous, I stop, switch back on my track, 'Surely there are *other ways . . .*'

She looks into the teapot, announces grandly, 'I'm not discussing tactics with you.'

'Can't you work on them from the inside or something?'

225

She is pouring my cup. 'Oh, *very* valiant, Mother.'

I splash milk into hers, muttering, '*Oh*, I didn't realize that this was about being *valiant*.'

'Look,' she pushes mine towards me, 'you're having a go at the wrong person. Go and have a go at Mr Gray.'

So I try to explain, 'I'm not *having-a-go*, Sylvie . . .'

She returns to her elbows, but lightly, and looks directly into my eyes. 'Let me guess: this is for my own good.'

'Well, *yes* . . .'

'Listen,' she gives up, starts on her own cup, '*that school* pushed me to this.'

I smile, but brittle, 'Funny how the only push that *that school* gives *everyone else* is to college or university.' I have strayed into another well-worn dispute.

On cue, without even looking up, she counters, 'I've told you, I'm not going to college-or-university.'

Quickly back to the point: 'Can't you just apologize to Mr Gray?' I know that people say that I am too easy on Sylvie: but *I* say that I want an easy life. And, anyway, what is the point of being hard?

She tells me, 'No.'

'Just for having said "fuck"?' I would never, usually, say the word; but there is no point in euphemism, she tends not to respect euphemism.

But not even a smile, or a peep of a smile, from her. 'No. I meant every word.'

I implore, '*Sylvie* . . .'

And suddenly she flares, 'It would make no difference, he *hates* me.'

I soothe, 'He doesn't *hate* you, darling; no one hates you.' I reach for the tin of biscuits, a Christmas present from Auntie

Sarah, and ponder the lid: *Circumstances may cause us to vary the assortment from that illustrated.*

She remains fierce, 'He *does* hate me.'

Sometimes I suspect that she *wants* to think that people hate her. I cast around and come up with, 'He has a very difficult job to do – which he *can't* do if you're occupying his office.' I try to tweek a smile from her with my own: 'Hmm?' *See?*

But she is blind to this, she is off: 'Why is everyone on at me, all the time? Why did you have to mention university again, just now?'

'I *didn't*.'

'You *did*.'

'When?'

'Just now.'

And suddenly I remember. 'Oh, yes. I'm sorry.'

She yelps, 'You're *not* sorry.'

Which, of course, is true. I simply *said* that I was sorry, without thinking. Now I can think no further than, 'Look, we have to decide what to do about Mr Gray, but for now I'm rather tired, so I'm going to have a bath.'

When I reach the door, she pipes, 'I mean, why *should* I go to university?'

I can see that a fresh pile of junk mail has landed in the hallway. 'Well, why not?'

Behind me, she is reasoning, 'I mean, I *could* go, *easily*.'

'*Well* then.'

Darkly, she says, 'That's not a reason.'

'Oh, Sylvie . . .' I give up on my bath, momentarily, to explain, 'I simply want you to be happy.'

This seems to cause her to have trouble with a mouthful

of tea, and to slam her cup on to the table. 'And the way to be happy is to read more books?'

'It'll be different from school.' Is this true? And how do *I* know? 'And, anyway, is *work* fun?'

She scowls, mutters, '*You* seem to think so.'

'Yes, well, but we're very different.' She cannot possibly argue with this.

But she looks at me, and I do not know what the look says, yes or no. Then she tries, '*You* didn't go away to college: so, were *you* happy?' There is more than a hint of a challenge in this. But then, everything comes as a challenge, from her. I think that the question is genuine, that she wants an answer.

And I would like to answer, but how?

'I *think* so.'

Because looking back, scanning speedily, all that comes to mind is *facts*; well, no, not *facts*, but friends, family, jobs, homes, holidays, even clothes. People and places and objects, rather than states of mind and emotions. From a distance, all states of mind and emotions seem like one another: perhaps there are only so many, and I am old enough to have had them all.

'My problem, as you know, was that I married badly.'

She concedes with a sort of swoon of her eyebrows: unfortunately, she knows how badly, from her lifetime of access visits.

'Anyway,' I try to finish convincingly, 'life was different, in those days: we expected less.'

And instantly I doubt the truth of this: certainly *I* expected less; but there were some girls, like Caroline Jacobs and Beth Stanford in my class, and those women who have become Sylvie's teachers, who aimed further.

Sylvie says, 'Perhaps you expected *more*, if you expected a life in the home to be enough.'

I have never thought of it that way. But this is how it is with Sylvie: some people tell me that she thinks too much of herself, by which they mean that she thinks too little of *them*, but at least she *thinks*.

She seems to want to say no more, so I fill the silence: 'I was never very bookish, I liked a laugh.' And I bracket an aside with a nervous laugh: 'Still do, of course.'

She is drawing lines with a fingertip in the condensation on the milk bottle.

I continue, 'I was never the type for university.' And for no particular reason, I laugh again. But she tuts, loudly. I do not know why, perhaps she has a point of view on this, one of those points of view of hers, one of the many: perhaps she thinks that we are all the type for university, that university is not for a certain type. A contradiction in terms, surely, because university is for those who are special. And I was never special. Which was fine by me. 'I would never have wanted to wear one of those black things on my head, black has always tended to bring out my bags.'

She fails to laugh in return. In fact, she looks so baffled that I have to examine the pack of toothpaste on top of the mound of shopping: *Children should use a pea-sized amount and be supervised.*

How was my childhood? Thinking back, my childhood seems to have been about my brother. *He* is all that I remember of my childhood, perhaps because he was bigger than me. When I was small, I did everything that he said. And when he grew up and spent less time with me, I did very little. I had friends, of course; still have them, still have many of them. *He* went away to college. Geography. And now he is a teacher, which is how I know that Mr Gray's job is so difficult. I never considered that education was for me, but was this because I was a girl, or younger, or just *me*? How do I know? Why should I care, now? My mother worked in a nursery school and my father was a proofreader, they believed in education, never said or implied that education was not for me. I think that they would have been happy for me to continue. Happier, I am sure, than they were for me to marry Bernie. Bernie was my mistake, my only mistake.

Suddenly, she speaks: 'I might have a baby.' And now she looks up, into my eyes, as if there was a question somewhere in these words.

I hurry to reassure her, 'You have all the time in the world for babies,' and explain, 'I suppose that what I want is for you to have all the options, to keep your options open.'

But in the same wide-eyed, wondering way, she says, 'To have a baby seems quite a nice option.'

And, ridiculously, I repeat, as if it is a refrain from a lullaby, 'All the time in the world.'

But she continues, '*Compared*,' and she has turned fierce, 'compared to a life of being *graded*.'

I laugh this off: 'You wait, because when you have a baby, your health visitor is only too happy to do the honours, believe me.'

But which, from her look, she fails to do. Then she recovers her composure and tells me, urges, 'I want to be a *real person*.'

'Oh, you're most definitely that.'

Then she repeats, 'I might have a baby.'

Suddenly, I see that this is not necessarily a theoretical discussion.

She continues, 'I mean, I *could.*'

Instinct sits me down, makes me voice the question: 'Are you pregnant?'

'*No!*' But now her fierce features flatten into calmness. 'All I'm saying is that I *could* have a baby, if I *choose.*'

'*Choose?*' Why do I feel that she is threatening me? My gaze catches on her hand, on the tabletop: the bones of her little hand, tinder and marbles tied in muslin.

'I'm sixteen,' she is petulant.

I counter, 'Barely. Do you know how to be careful?' Inexplicably, I am angry with her. This is not how I am supposed to feel, how I planned to feel; this is quite simply *not me.* Anger achieves nothing. And now, suddenly, I am so much more worse: 'You probably don't believe in contraception, do you? Something to do with animals, with tests, or something.'

She says, 'That's *ridiculous.*'

Or I think that this is what she said, but I am too busy saying, 'And as for *abortion.*'

'Ah, well, *yes,*' she says, *now you're talking.*

Which stops me in my tracks.

She leans forward, presses down onto her forearms; her upper ribs ripple like piano keys. 'I'm not altogether happy with the thought of abortion.'

Not *altogether happy?* with the *thought* of?

'Well, *don't* think, then; it's not something that you *think* about, it's something that you *need to do*, and let's hope that you – '

' – I mean, not *these* days,' she has stopped listening to me. So I stress, 'Women *died.*'

But her eyes find mine and she says, 'And nowadays *babies* die.' This is not said fervently, but faintly, more like a question. And now she tries, 'Look, I'm not saying . . .' and tries again, 'but these days women aren't *dependent* . . .' She stops suddenly, shrugs: *do you see?*

I do not know, I do not know. As usual, she has run rings around me. I squeeze shut my eyes, press my fingertips on to my temples. Slowly, I decide, 'I should have a word with Dunc.' Her boyfriend.

She squeaks, 'Leave Dunc out of this! He has nothing to do with this.'

'Oh, so if you decide to have your baby, then you're going to go for self-insemination, are you?'

Thin-lipped, she merely manages, '*God*, you're disgusting.' But then she accelerates into, 'You don't *own* me, you're like some medieval . . .' before she flusters, fails, falls into silence.

I am curious. 'Medieval what?'

'Medieval *father*.' All the insult came with *father*.

'I have something to tell you.' There: *done*.

For years, I have had something to tell her. For her whole life. Now she has forced my hand.

'Yes?' Now she is curious, but she remains arch.

I am so relieved to have broached the subject that I have forgotten that I have not actually told her. I ease myself in: 'Something about your father.'

Her eyes slide away. 'Oh, *him*.'

This is a help, because I can say, 'No, not him; I mean, he's not your father.' There: *said*. I exhale, but unfortunately feel full of air, blown.

Her eyes slide back to mine. She wonders, 'My father's not my father,' without conviction. She is eyeing me with suspicion, she suspects that I am senile.

'Biologically speaking,' I confirm, 'someone else is your father.'

'Who?' she asks, levelly.

Which takes me by surprise. 'Who?'

'Yes, who?'

'You want to know who?' And not how it happened, or whether anyone knows?

'Yes, *I want to know who*.' Her face has become a tough little shell, a husk; her eyes, two marks; her mouth, a mere fracture. 'What did you *think* that I'd want to know?' And, quietly, she urges, '*Who*.'

How do I answer? Because the name will mean nothing to her. 'Well, you don't know him.'

'Well, *who is he*, then?' But I can see that this – *you don't know him* – did mean something to her: she had been thinking of the men who were around when she was a child, who were our friends – her Uncles Vic and John and Len and the others – she had been thinking of them as possible candidates.

Horrified, I cannot stop myself, '*You thought Uncle Vic or Uncle John –* ?'

Suddenly she is screaming, 'Well, *I don't know what to think, do I? Because you're not telling me.*' Her hands are moving in the air, she is throwing off fury like a Catherine wheel. 'What do you *mean*, I don't know him? Did *you* know him? It's a *simple enough question, surely*. Or was it the *milkman* or someone?'

I collect myself, stand up, back off. 'Now you're *trivializing* this.'

She fails to let up, and, indeed, seems to rise in her chair, to follow me: '*Me? You* found it so trivial that you managed to overlook it for *sixteen years*.'

'*Quite* the contrary,' which, if she had stopped to think, if she had tried to be fair, she would have realized.

Now she slows down, but only for sarcasm: 'I *mean*, why tell me *now*? In fact, why don't we pretend that the last few minutes never happened, and slip back into blissful ignorance?'

Glancing at the bottle of tonic in my jumble of shopping, my gaze skids over the small print on the label: *Open away from people and fragile objects.* I push on: 'I'm telling you for a reason.'

She puffs, 'Oh, a *reason*: other than the reason that I have a right to know my own father, you mean?'

'He had a gene.'

This freezes her. Then, 'What?' slaps the stony silence.

I know that she does not mean anything like, *What is a gene?* She is a clever girl, she knows about genes, knows what this means.

'If you're going to have children, you should know about the gene.'

Without moving a muscle, not even of her mouth, she is hurrying me: 'Which gene?'

I will have to say the words, *One of his children*: words which I have never said aloud.

'One of his children had cystic fibrosis.' Then I rush to reassure her, 'One of his *three* children.' Only one.

She echoes, 'Cystic fibrosis,' cluelessly.

'Chest, mainly. Infections.'

Her eyes open up to me in a way that I have not seen for years: suddenly, once again, I am the source of all wisdom. 'Bad?'

And I have so often wondered: did she survive, did his little

234

girl survive? *Anya*. His children – *Lucy, Ed, Anya* – who are no longer children; who, by now, will be, should be, adults, nearly as old as we were when Sylvie was conceived.

'Yes, quite bad,' *really quite bad*; but I can push us on into the future: 'but the prospects are much better nowadays.'

But my reassurance fails to reach her, I can see no trace of it in her eyes. 'Do people die?'

And I have to concede defeat. 'Eventually, usually, yes.'

She is homing in. '*How* eventually?'

I do not know, I have to become more vague, 'Twenties? Thirties?' Before falling back on, 'But the outlook is improving.'

Suddenly she moves, to hook her hair behind an ear, ready for business. 'And you don't think that I have this disease?'

So, she has listened; she understands that this is not about her but about her children. 'You *don't* have; we would know.'

'Not even slightly? Are you sure?'

I almost laugh, because this is absurd: 'You think that I haven't spent your whole life watching for the slightest sign?' Quietly triumphant, I tell her, 'You've never even had a *cough*, you must be the only child in the world who has never had a cough.' My miracle child.

But she is somewhere else, on another track: 'And you still had me? You know I could have this cystic fibrosis, but you still had me, you took a chance?'

I can tell that she is not trying to make a point, to hark back to our earlier dispute; she is merely thinking aloud. But, of course, in those days, I would have had no choice: she has failed to realize this, and I swallow my shock at her naïvety. *Would* a choice have made any difference? How do I know, how can I know, now? 'It's *chest infections*, darling, not . . .'

but I stop myself from trying to compile a catalogue of birth defects. 'Anyway, I didn't know: I knew that his little girl had this disease, but I didn't know that it was hereditary, not for years, not until I read something, once.'

Once? How many times, in the end? I remember the moment when I first saw the words: Sylvie was framed in the doorway, on the patio in her pyjamas in the early summer dusk, playing with a doll. In front of me, on the coffee table, I had a cup of milky coffee, a Nice biscuit bridging the saucer. Flopped in my lap, a women's magazine, the *True Life Story* patched with photos of a mother and her two daughters, three women in sequence, the whole family displayed like dismantled Russian dolls. On the patio, Sylvie's voice bubbled low in the thick air, in the dregs of the day; she was telling off her doll: *Naughty . . . naughty . . .* She was relishing this word, bowed over the doll, intimate, and full of admiration. Slowly, my moment extended to the biscuit, which was not quite as crisp as it should have been, and deliciously so: fractionally slow to yield to my front teeth; instantly sticky in my mouth. Then I started on the story: *Doreen Jenkins' daughter Samantha has cystic fibrosis, a disease which runs in families . . .* My head jerked up, punched back into the leatherette of the sofa. *Runs in families.* There, in front of me, cross-legged on the dim crazy paving, was my family: Sylvie, as clean and constant as a night-light.

I knew that there was nothing wrong with her. *Nothing.* But, sitting there, I held my breath and listened, tried to track *her* breaths: I lay in wait for any shudder of phlegm, for any cold silver tinkle down in her tubes. I cringed in anticipation of the cough which she would shoot up into the falling darkness. The cough which would give her away. But nothing. As usual. Nothing but the relentless turning of air through those tough lungs. Then, suddenly she had scampered to her feet, her dry soles struck on the stones. I looked away from her eyes, looked down, back to the story. And if I had not read on, I would never have known. Because I knew nothing of genes, of how they can lie hidden; how a bad gene nestles with normal genes, only to be teased out, later, by an accomplice, to make a mark on another generation. I read on, and learned that Doreen Jenkins' other daughter did not have the disease, but could not be sure that her own children would be born healthy. Odd, now, to think that if Doreen Jenkins had not had the daughter who was dying, then I would not have realized the danger in my own.

I hurry to tell Sylvie, 'And then I read everything that I could find.' I did my homework.

Immediately, she puts this to the test: 'So, then, what are my chances?' Her chin is jutted to receive the blow.

I have the figures at the ready: 'If you *do* have the gene, and you *meet* someone who has the gene – ' *meet?* another euphemism ' – then any children that you have will have a one in four chance of having cystic fibrosis.'

Very quickly, she asks, 'How many people have the gene?'

I tell her, 'You can test for the gene,' before I answer her question. 'One in twenty,' then I add, 'and they can test your baby before it's born, to see if it *is* a one-in-four.'

And this is the whole truth, this is everything that I can tell her.

The floorboards flutter as a passing car booms a beat which is louder than a loud-hailer; than election promises.

'Listen to that,' I say, pointlessly.

Tentatively, she asks, 'Is that a lot, one in twenty?'

237

Is it? 'I don't know.'

For quite some time, I have been standing, leaning on to the back of my chair, sometimes heavily. Now I move around the chair and sit down.

She frowns, and once again focuses upon, reaches for, the milk bottle. 'Why didn't he tell you that it was hereditary?' Her fingertips slide down the neck of the bottle, on the haze of moisture.

'Oh,' I have to put her straight, 'he never knew that I was pregnant.'

The fingers stop, her gaze snaps back into mine, the eyes blank but fierce because they are unfathomable, unanchored. 'How did he not know?'

Simple: 'He was my boss, I left my job,' left him with a lie, told him that Bernie had a new job and we were moving away. I do not know if he knew that it was a lie, because I did not look into his eyes when I told him. I had not looked into his eyes for three weeks. In fact, I had probably only ever looked into his eyes *once*, three weeks before, and *then* look what happened: Sylvie.

Who, now, laughs, 'Your *boss*, oh *God*, what a *cliché*.'

His eyes were nearly green but nearly transparent, simply the colour of whatever it is that eyes are: the colour of the soul, I suppose. A mere smoke of colour. A smoky soul. Not dissimilar to tarnished jade, and I knew the rule for jade: it has to be touched, worn, warmed, or it will darken. When I looked into his eyes, I saw that his soul had been darkening for years. I knew all about darkened souls.

'The occasional quick screw on his desk?'

She is laughing, but this is bravado, she is angry with me and I will have to sit this out.

I cannot stop myself, though, from a brief, prim defence, '*No.*' Not occasional. Not quick. Not on his desk, on no one's desk, there was no desk.

'You were having an *affair*, and then suddenly you *went*, and he never *wondered*?' *About you. About whether there was a me.* A peep of fury, now, from her carefully constructed calm, like a snapped twig in a piece of occupational health wickerwork.

'It wasn't an *affair* – '

' – *Oh,*' mock delight, 'a one-night stand: I'm the result of a one-night stand with some old sod in a suit? Better *and better.*'

I slam back in my chair, fold my arms, 'Whatever you prefer, Sylvie; whatever you want to think. Because I can tell that you're not going to listen to me; you already have your own little version.'

She creeps from her chair, but upwards; seems low, but leans over me, 'Now *you* listen to *me,*' her tone is the verbal equivalent of this position, an unnerving and compelling mix of high and low, 'I'll have the *truth*, please, because I've had sixteen years of a *lie.*' The brown irises have a green haze, but her eyes are too much her own to remind me of him: less a reminder, more a coincidence, like certain words in someone else's mouth, an expression which chimes a chord.

'You were wrong about the *old*: he was twenty-seven.' Of course, twenty-seven *is* old, to her; but I sense that when she referred to him as an *old-sod-in-a-suit*, she was working to a different scale, she was thinking of the beer-gutted model, forties or fifties. As if I would – I am not defending *him*, so much as *me*. 'And *sod*? No, he was a lovely man.'

'So lovely that he cheated on his wife.' She is back in her

chair, but up on her knees; she is small enough to be able to do this. She is sitting high, in sceptical judgement.

I mumble, 'Well, our marriages were really very rocky.' An understatement.

Suddenly she is down and closer, forearms on the table. 'What did you feel for him?' And I see that her eyes are twitchy with hopes.

This is quaintly old-fashioned: what did I *feel for him?* The memory is the sheer pain of my undeclared love: like glass in my skin – the more I tried to pick over and free myself, the worse the pain. I had to hope that, in time, I would shed the pieces; that as I grew old, I would grow new, too. And, in time, I did.

'Were you in love with him?'

'Oh, yes.'

'And now?'

'Now?' Beyond us, on the main road, there are sirens: a new variation, show-off sirens, several of them shaken up together, tumbling away, losing their rhythm.

'Yes, what do you feel for him *now?*'

'*Now?*' She wants the truth? 'Nothing.'

'*Nothing?*'

I can see that, as far as she is concerned, this is not how the story should run. But she wants the truth.

'Well, I *know* that I *was* in love with him, I *know* that he was *lovely*, but . . .' how can I explain this to her?

'You remember Billy Allen, when you were fourteen?' *Remember how, for a year, he was everything to you, you wrote his name over everything that you owned, traced his every movement, but now he is nothing, someone else's boyfriend, demoted from your dreams into real life, into the sleepwalk of everyday life?*

'Oh *come on*,' she winds herself back down into her chair, her arms around herself, 'that's hardly the same.'

'No? Neil was a long time ago. That time has gone.' I can see from her bristling shoulders that she regards this as callous. I will have to try hard to explain, 'Passion is not something that you can take with you.' *Try harder*, 'My love for him was never *written into* me, but was something that *happened* to me.' And this is the wonder, surely: that it happened at all. Because if I had looked the other way, if I had lived in another town, if I had failed to see the advert or not applied for the job ... the ifs are everywhere, running into one another, the full effect is like a cut diamond. But, something which *happens* will eventually *stop* happening. And I can live with that. 'He was a lovely man, he was lovely-looking, he was funny and kind. And by then, Bernie was a dead loss.'

This mention of Bernie prompts her. Cautiously, her arms still wound hard around herself, she shifts in her chair, settles, allows, 'Yeah, well,' *I can believe that.*

Then, 'His name was Neil?' Her eyes are wide to drink down whatever I can give her.

'Neil James.' No harm, surely, in telling her something as simple as his name, and such a simple name.

'Did he love *you*?' Suddenly she has leaned so far over the table that I have to move my cup. I know what her question means, I am not stupid: she wants to think that he would love her, too. She presses on, 'Did he ever say that he loved you?'

Since when did she ever believe what anyone *said*?

I am going to have to tell her the whole story: 'Look, we worked alone together in an office, all day long, day in, day out, for seven months.' This could be anyone's story, but now, to my surprise, my body begins to recall our laughter, a warmth like the sun on my back. There was no sun in our office because of the venetian blind, the dense ribs of the blind, yet an image is burned into my eyes, I do not know if it is under-exposed or over-exposed, but somehow the light is wrong, because there is *only* the light: the X-ray glow of the venetian blind, making moonlight in the day; and his shirt, far too white, fallen to slack folds around his forearms. But even if I squeeze my eyes shut, I cannot quite reach the forearms, cannot quite slide into the space between the cotton and his skin, into the air which is warmed by him, the air on which, in which, he moves.

When I had to go away from him, to go home in the evenings or for the weekends, I felt that I was holding my breath, I was merely holding onto life. And when I saw him again, the next day, or on Mondays, that air came spilling from me. There was never quite enough air in me, or going through me. When I went away from him for ever, I felt that I was going down into a black airless hole to die.

'But anyway,' back to the story, for Sylvie, to her story, the story of her, 'we went to a conference, where we had to stay overnight.'

She stops chewing a nail to remark, sourly, 'Don't tell me, he made his expense account work hard on you in the bar.'

'Very late, I went up to his room and knocked on his door.'

Going up to his room was like going up onto the roof, and knocking on his door was like throwing myself off. I did not know that he would catch me, but he did. I sliced through my life, and he broke my fall.

The wet nail hovers, shining, but her mouth is a hard dry line which cracks just enough to complain, 'So, why did you walk away?'

'Because very soon I knew that I was going to have you.' I had become pregnant on the last day of my cycle: a miracle baby, almost.

'How do you know which one is my father?'

'I knew that you had nothing to do with Bernie because, for quite a while, *I* had had nothing to do with Bernie.' Smiling my apology for this euphemism, I wince inwardly to think how I had had to cover my tracks: I had to seduce Bernie. 'I was going to have you, so I needed to stay married.'

She wails, 'To the wrong man?' The line has flown from her mouth but landed on her eyebrows.

'I was *married*. *He* was married.'

She squeezes out a whine, '*So?*'

'Apart from anything else, he had three children. And one of them was very ill. And if I had broken up one or both of our marriages, what would have happened to us? I would never have managed on my own, there was no maternity leave or equal pay or anything. *His* wife would never have managed on *her* own, and what about those children? Marriage was different, in those days; marriage kept women and children *alive*. You did *not* break up a marriage, your own or anyone else's. What we did was bad, but was nothing, compared . . .'

Sunk back down onto the nail, she slurs, 'Three years later, you *did* divorce.'

'Ah, well, yes, three years later,' when I was able to manage. But was this a miscalculation, my second mistake? To have stayed with Bernie for those few years? Should I have taken a chance and gone? My mistakes gather around Bernie like flies.

She seems to haul her head from her nail, holds her head very high to send the accusation, 'You must hate me for mucking up your life.'

My heart turns over and sends up a laugh, which I quash, but which unfortunately leaks out as a titter, 'You're *kidding*, aren't you? You were the one wonderful consequence of the whole mess.' She will have to take my word for this: one of my hands has flown as far as the table, but twitches, terrified to go after her. 'I cut my losses, but I didn't lose: I had you.'

Her eyes remain narrow, her tone considered, 'And you know what I hate *you* for, don't you?'

Ice blooms over my heart, 'Oh, please, Syl, *don't . . .*'

Her eyes contract, hard, 'How *could* you?' And she spirals, 'My *whole life*, you led me to believe that *fucking bastard –* '

I come down hard on her, '*Don't* call him a bastard, Sylvie, he's your . . .' father? I stop, just in time.

And now what do I say? Back to the beginning: 'I felt that you needed a father.' Everyone felt that everyone needed a father, in those days. Everyone felt that anyone was better than no one.

'But I *had* a father.' Fury has crushed her chin into dimples.

'No,' I have to try to explain, 'he was just a man who – '

'*Couldn't say no?*' She is up, and whirled to the window.

I grab the milk bottle, to cool my hands. 'You know your problem, Sylvie? You're witty and charming, but rarely simultaneously.'

She turns to me. 'He never knew about me, you never gave him a chance. You played God.'

'*Someone* had to.' *You try to do better*: there was no one for me, I had to carry my secret on my own, I was alone in my impossibly crowded life, my crowded body. My whole life hung in the balance – *two* lives – and there was no one to help me.

She is calmer, her fury swallowed, a mere stain of a sulk on her mouth. 'Does *no one* know?' I shake my head but she persists: 'Not even a friend? Or, I don't know, the doctor or someone?'

'No one.' I sigh, drained. 'Just you and me, babe.'

'And *only* just, in my case.' A pause before she asks, 'Were you always going to tell me?'

'I was *always* going to tell you.'

'What will I do when I see him?'

Him, Bernie: I am up from my chair before I realize, and commanding, '*Nothing*,' I cannot allow her to do this, to change the story of my life, to write me off like this.

But she hardly sees me, she is musing, 'How will I *feel*?'

Without taking my eyes from her, I return to my chair. How *will* she *feel*? Good question. 'Much as I have always done, I suppose.'

A spark in her glance, '*Too right* I'm not going to say anything to him,' and a switch of a smile, 'because I don't want him to refuse to pay my grant if I *do* decide to go to college.'

I run a milk-cooled hand over my forehead and into my too-dry hair. 'Rather mercenary, Sylvie.'

And she gives me a look which puts me in my place. 'A matter of survival.'

She comes over, back into her chair, where she hovers. 'So . . .' Her elbows planted on the table, her face in a tulip of hands, she smiles. Conspiratorial? Or the lull before the kill? '. . . where do I find Mr Neil James?'

'You don't.' He moved a lot with work, he could have moved anywhere, even abroad.

'*Oh*,' the smile widens, 'don't you worry, I'll find him.'

Worry? How odd that I never anticipated this: that she would want to trace him. Because *I* did not want to trace him? I *thought* that I had thought of us as very different, but now I realize that I have always known how very similar we are: we are both practical, turned hard towards the future. We differ in our methods. So I know that this desire to unearth her origins is utterly out of character. I start to warn her off, '*No . . .*'

A wash of dismay over her pearl of a face, 'He's my father,' followed by a return of the smile, but brief, conclusive: *fact*.

But this is not wholly true, '*Is* he? He *was* your father for a few hours, in a hotel room, nearly seventeen years ago, and wherever he is now, he has a *life*, he has a *wife*,' actually, I do not know if he has a wife, nowadays, or the *same* wife, 'and *children*.' I do not even know how many children, how many have grown up. And he may even have *grandchildren*. What I do know, now, is that Sylvie and I have always lived in accord, that this push and pull of ours has been a pendulum, we have held each other in check but moved each other forward through the years. And now she is poised to throw us out of sync, to turn back the clock, to change our past. What will this do to our future?

She is not going to do this, because I am going to stop her.

'If you turn up now, Sylvie, you make their whole lives a lie, you ruin their lives for the sake of – ' *I have to say this, in her own words* ' – a quick screw.' This will do for the truth, for now.

Her mouth opens, but apparently involuntarily because she says nothing.

So I continue, 'How can you spend your days trying to prove that parents don't matter, and then decide to do this?' I try to be calm: confrontation is not the way, or not *my* way.

I have lived so many years with the image of us in opposition to each other, but now I see that this is not so: she is *in my hands*. I can stop her, I can hold her, I can hold fast. In my whole life I have never fought for anything or anyone, but I have the strength, saved up. I will win. I will work on her, I will turn her around and win her over. Looking at her, and contemplating my options, the advice which was a blur above her head for those ten minutes on the bus comes clear in my mind's eye: *Don't touch it, Don't ignore it, Stay calm.*